"You looked wary for a minute there."

Tori gazed up at the vertical stone formation. "Just overwhelmed by old memories."

"You sure that's all?"

Her smile faded to a guilt-ridden grin. "It's been a long time since I've been here. I was highly tempted to head back to my grandparents' house before anyone saw me."

Tori's sudden insecurity intrigued Steve. If she didn't want to see everyone, why had she agreed to come? He wanted more than anything to believe her reason included him, but he wouldn't take that for granted, either. "Before you change your mind, why not say hello?" Steve touched his hand to the small of her back, encouraging her to join the festivities.

Books by Carol Steward

Love Inspired

There Comes a Season #27
Her Kind of Hero #56
Second Time Around #92
Courting Katarina #134
This Time Forever #165
Finding Amy #263
Finding Her Home #282

CAROL STEWARD

wrote daily to a pen pal for ten years, yet writing as a career didn't occur to her for another two decades. "My first key chain said 'Bloom Where You're Planted.' I've tried to follow that advice ever since."

Carol, her husband and their three children have planted their roots in Greeley. Together, their family enjoys sports, camping and discovering Colorado's beauty. Carol has operated her own cake-decorating business and spent fifteen years providing full-time child care to more than one hundred children before moving on to the other end of the education field. She is now an admissions advisor at a state university.

As always, Carol loves to hear from her readers. You can contact her at P.O. Box 200269, Evans, CO 80620. She would also love for you to visit her Web page at www.carolsteward.com.

FINDING HER HOME

CAROL STEWARD

Steeple
Hill®

Published by Steeple Hill Books™

STEEPLE HILL BOOKS

Steeple
Hill®

ISBN 0-373-87292-5

FINDING HER HOME

Copyright © 2004 by Carol Steward

www.SteepleHill.com

Printed in U.S.A.

The LORD said to me, "Do not say, 'I am only a boy'; for you shall go to all to whom I send you, and you shall speak whatever I command you."

—*Jeremiah* 1:7

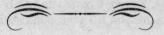

Dedicated to *all* teachers and educators,
but mostly to my late grandmother, Mildred Call,
my sisters, Cindy and Cynde Bohannan,
my late brother-in-law, Dan Correll, and the
Steward family of educators, Mildred, Jack, Marty,
Dave, Doug, Karen, Charles and Deb Haverfield.
Thank you for your dedication!

Chapter One

"It's four-thirty in the morning. Who would be calling at this time of day?" Tori Sandoval picked up the phone, startled to hear her grandfather's voice. "*¿Abuelo?* Calm down. What's wrong?"

"Victoria, *Abuela* collapsed. The doctor at the clinic is having her flown to Pikes Peak Hospital. Can you meet her there?"

"Of course. What happened? How is she?" Tori choked back tears, allowing his announcement to sink in.

Tori heard Grandfather sob. "She fell…" he said, pausing to blow his nose. He rambled on, telling every detail. "I had to call the paramedics. I couldn't do anything for her."

"That's their job. You shouldn't be lifting her. Are you okay?"

"Fine. I'll drive up after sunrise."

Tori sat up in bed, the thought of her eighty-two-year-old grandfather making the 150-mile drive alone completed the wake-up process instantly. "No! I'll come get you."

"*Abuela* needs you. I'll take it slow and do just fine. The nurse says my Maria will be in the hospital a while. You get to the hospital now, angel. Don't worry about me."

"*¡Abuelo!*"

Silence.

Thirty minutes later Tori Sandoval pressed the brakes of her four-wheel drive as she entered the al-ready-busy hospital parking lot.

She parked the vehicle then punched in the number on her cell phone. "Sheriff Martinez, this is Victoria Sandoval…."

"Victoria, I'm sorry about your grandmother. I'm trying to find someone to bring Jose to Colorado Springs. He shouldn't be driving in town, let alone on the highway."

Relief washed over her. "Yes, I know. That's what I'm calling about. I could come get him if you could stop him…."

"Don't worry about coming here. I'll make sure Jose gets a ride." They spoke a few minutes longer and she gave Sheriff Martinez her cell phone number in case he needed to reach her.

"You holler if you need anything. We'll keep a close watch on the house."

"Thanks, Sheriff." Tori disconnected the call and stuffed the phone into her briefcase. "*Abuela* and *Abu-*

elo need to realize it's time for them to move here so I can help out more," she said aloud to herself. "I can't move to Segundo now, I'm so close to finishing my thesis, and school's just starting…."

Tori rushed across the parking lot and through the automatic doors to the emergency room. She stepped up to the counter. "Excuse me, my grandmother was being transported here from Segundo Emergency Clinic. Is Maria Sandoval here yet?"

"Let me go check."

The nurse returned a few minutes later, shaking her head. "Her flight was delayed. If you'll have a seat in the waiting room, we'll call you when she arrives."

"Any idea how she is?"

The middle-aged woman smiled. "She's stable. We'll send her directly to the neurology center."

"Thank you." Tori nodded numbly and turned to find a seat. After assessing the lack of available space, she decided to wait outside. Maybe the fresh air would help to clear her mind. She walked back to her vehicle before realizing she'd left her bagel on the table next to the door at her condo. "So much for breakfast."

She had known this time would come, when her grandparents would need more care than was available in Coal Valley. Tori closed her eyes, questions racing through her head a dozen at a time. She glanced at her watch again. Time stood still.

Stable. What did that mean exactly? Had her grandfather reached the rest of the family? Now what? Mom and Dad can't come home for months. Aunt Juanita is still recovering from chemo treatments. I can't take care of them in Segundo.

Tori saw the cross on the hospital sign and cringed. She hadn't been a regular church attendee in years, but her grandparents didn't miss a week. Surely God wouldn't turn a deaf ear. *Lord, be with* Abuela *and give her strength, and help the sheriff find someone to bring* Abuelo *here.* Pacing the sidewalk to ward off the early morning chill, she twisted her watch around her wrist and noted that less than five minutes had passed.

Opening her planner, Tori checked her schedule. Orientation with the new teachers. School improvement plan with building administrators—skip. Attendance forms—format. Tori rubbed her temple, making new notes for the day.

Half an hour passed before she heard the stutter of a helicopter's approach. A bright pink glow painted the horizon and spilled across the sky as the copter landed on the hospital roof. Tori returned to the waiting room in time to hear her name called. She was then directed to an examining room where she introduced herself to the medics. Then she turned to her grandmother. "*Abuela,* it's Tori." Her grandmother didn't respond. The left side of her mouth drooped. Her skin looked gray despite the oxygen tube under her nose.

"Is she okay?" Tori whispered to the medics.

"She's stable. She became agitated when we moved her into the copter. We delayed the flight until she calmed down again. She was worried about your grandfather driving here."

Tori smiled. "That's been taken care of. He has a ride."

"Good. It's not easy separating loved ones at times like this." The paramedics rolled the gurney into the service elevator and pushed it to one side. "Come on. We'll save you the trouble of finding us again." Tori patted *Abuela*'s hand, alarmed that it didn't move. Tori felt the tears sting her eyes. She followed in silence while they settled *Abuela* into a room.

The nurse introduced herself and offered to wait until Tori's grandfather arrived to complete the check-in. Tori answered what questions she could, sure *Abuelo* would be worried and tired when he got to town. He'd already gone through the "check in and wait" routine at the Segundo clinic.

Staff came in and left the room, but *Abuela* didn't stir. "Is it normal for her to sleep so much?" Tori asked the nurse.

"Very. The neurologist will run tests soon." She adjusted a small clamp on *Abuela*'s finger and waited for the new reading. "Her oxygen is improving."

Tori tried to think of questions to ask, but only one mattered. "Will *Abuela* be okay?"

The nurse finished recording the numbers flashing on the monitors then motioned for Tori to follow her out to the hallway. In a hushed tone, the nurse apologized that she couldn't give a definite answer. "The tests will give us a better idea of the extent of the damage she's suffered. I know this isn't the answer you want, but I'm afraid that only time will tell. Maria appears to be a strong, active woman. That helps."

Three hours later Tori finally gave in to the nurse's urging and went to the cafeteria for some breakfast. She balanced a fruit yogurt cup and a frothy-topped caramel latte, struggling to keep her purse on her shoulder. She turned in to her grandmother's room and ran into a solid male body, bathing him in caramel, cream and mixed berries.

"Whoa. That gives an all-new meaning to 'freshly brewed coffee.'"

Tori looked at the man and dropped the cup. "Ah, ah," Tori gasped, stumbling on the slick floor as she stepped back. "Oh, my, I'm so sorry, Doctor. I didn't see you."

The man with salt-and-pepper hair, a deep tan and whiskey-brown eyes caught her by the arm and steadied her. "Careful."

She studied the mess trickling down his faded denim shirt and jeans. "I am so sorry. Did it burn you?"

"It's...warm." His eyes drifted to her pink polo shirt. "But I don't think there are any serious burns. How about you?"

She hadn't even realized her splatter was a mirror image of his. Looking up, she suddenly felt very...warm, as well. "I'll be fine. The nurse insisted I get something to eat, that you wouldn't be back again until Grandfather arrived."

A smile teased his lips. "I think there's some confusion...."

"Tori," her grandfather said a little too loudly, "this is Steven Remington from Stonewall Ranch. But I guess you already know that since you arranged for him to bring me here."

"*¡Abuelo!*" She glanced at the man she'd assumed was a doctor, then stepped over the mess, allowing Steven Remington's hand to steady her as she walked around the bed to hug her grandfather. "When did you get here?"

"Just a bit ago, angel." He took her face in his hands and kissed her forehead. "I'll take a rain check for a proper hug after you've cleaned up. Steven isn't a doctor. He teaches math at Coal Valley High and helps his uncle at the ranch. It was right fine of him to bring me here so *mi esposa* has a few of her own things." Tears filled *Abuelo*'s eyes. His voice softened as he spoke to his wife in their native language.

Tori looked from her grandfather to the man she was supposed to know, but didn't. She stepped back around the bed and stared at Mr. Remington, puzzled. "I'm sorry. I thought you were another doctor. Have we met before?"

"I don't think we've had that pleasure. Sheriff Martinez knew I was headed to the Springs today to pick up supplies, and asked me to give your grandfather a ride." He turned slightly and whispered to her. "I think Jose's pride is a little scorched this morning, not being trusted to drive himself here."

Tori nodded, understanding Grandpa's prickly mood. "I can imagine." She picked a fresh strawberry from her shirt and dropped it into the trash, trying to hide the tears that she'd just managed to dry before she'd entered the room. "Thank you so much for your kindness—" she hesitated "—Steven." The name fit him perfectly. Suave and sophisticated. Rugged, yet classy. "As I'm sure you guessed, I'm Tori Sandoval, Jose and Maria's clumsy granddaughter."

Steven knelt down to add more fruit to the trash can, and rose with a sympathetic smile. "I doubt that. Your mind was on more important matters, is all." He turned to the sink and pulled a handful of paper towels from the rack, handing several to Tori. "I'll see if the nurse has a mop for the floor. Be careful."

Tori cleaned herself as much as she could, only managing to mash the berries further into the fabric. Before Steven returned, Tori picked up the chunks of fruit and globs of yogurt from the floor.

Grandmother woke and tried to talk, but gibberish was all that came out. Grandpa's eyes watered. He took her hand in his as she struggled to get the words right. She shook her head and started over, the words garbled.

"Don't try to talk now, honey. Just rest. I'm not going anywhere. Steven Remington brought me, so I don't even have our own car here." Grandpa leaned over, tenderly kissed his wife's frail lips and she struggled to smile.

Abuela's body relaxed and her gaze shifted to Steven as he walked back into the room.

"Housekeeping will be in shortly with a mop," Steven said quietly as he stepped closer to Tori. "The nurse said the doctor will be right in, as well."

"Zlevem," *Abuela* said. She frowned. "Zte-vem...gwashias." The frown turned to fear. She pounded the bed with her good hand.

Tori started to interpret but stopped when Steven took Maria's hand. "You're welcome, Mrs. Sandoval. I'm happy to help."

Grandpa spoke, again, so loud that the entire wing of the hospital could probably hear him. "Steven is Bill's nephew. Remember, the one who came from out East to raise his *niños?*"

Steve almost blushed.

Abuela nodded, then looked at Tori and tried to lift her eyebrows. "Towee."

Tori stepped to the bedside as Steven moved, making room for her next to him, as Grandmother wouldn't let go of his hand.

A rap on the door caught everyone's attention. An older man wearing a white lab coat and stethoscope entered, followed by Grandmother's nurse.

"Good morning. I'm the neurologist—Dr. Kim-ball—and you may have met her nurse already." He turned to Tori and Steven and smiled. "Leila, it looks like we have another case of hospital-food-itis. Would you get a set of scrubs for these two to change into so they'll be a little more comfortable." Tori felt ridiculous for mistaking Steven for a doctor once she noticed Dr. Kimball's white coat and stethoscope.

The nurse left the room, and the housekeeper came in with the mop and bucket, cleaning while the doctor continued to fill the family in on *Abuela*'s condition, explaining in tedious detail what tests she would be having and why. "Right now, Maria, you seem to be doing very well. The tests will confirm the preliminary diagnosis and guide us in the best path to take in your rehabilitation."

Nurse Leila returned with a pair of scrubs for both Tori and Steven. Steven tried to give them back, explaining that he needed to get to his errands.

"I'd really like all of you to be here for the test results. We should be done in an hour or two. While the aides take Mrs. Sandoval down for the tests, Leila will show Mr. Sandoval to the waiting room. I'll get back to you as soon as possible."

"Dr. Kimball, I live a few miles away. Could we go clean up and get a bite to eat—Steven won't need to be here for the results."

"You go," Grandpa interrupted, "but I'm not leaving Maria. She may need me." He dropped into the chair next to the bed, and no amount of reasoning could change his mind. Even Maria's feeble attempts to plead with her husband failed.

"Sure, you should have time to run home and clean up, and we'll be sure to keep in touch with your grandfather." The doctor left the room, followed by the nurse.

"Victoria Isabelle!" her grandfather's deep voice rumbled.

"What?" Tori jumped and her stomach growled.

"Surely you aren't going to make Steven run his errands in stained clothes, are you?" He paused only a second before continuing. "You've been here for hours.

Why don't you go on home and get both of your clothes washed before those stains set in."

Steven shook his head. "I'll be fine, really."

"Nonsense," her grandfather stated, "It looks as if the two of you took a dive into the punch bowl. Don't worry about us. You get something to eat, clean up and take care of Steven. Can't send a man on his way looking like that."

Tori wanted to fade like a mirage on the desert. In addition to being sticky, she was tired, hungry and anxious to find out more about *Abuela*'s condition. None of which were going to get any attention sitting in a waiting room. "Yes, sir. I'll be back soon." She kissed her grandparents, picked up her bags and headed out the door as the staff arrived to take her grandmother for tests.

Steven followed. Halfway down the hall he broke the silence. "You don't need to concern yourself with my clothes with all you have on your mind, Tori."

"I don't know what's wrong with me. I should have suggested it earlier. *Abuelo*'s right. I couldn't send you to the store looking like that." She dug through her bag searching for her keys, rattling on about where she'd parked. "You can follow me to my condo. It's not more than ten minutes away."

"I can pick up another set of clothes. It's no big deal, really. I'm not afraid of a mess…or being seen like this. You, on the other hand, know people here and have a reputation to uphold as principal of the prestigious high school."

"Assistant principal of a middle school, and I never—"

"You didn't have to." A twinkle lit his almond-shaped eyes, and Tori considered why her grandpa had suddenly become so insistent about her leaving with Steven. "Your grandfather didn't stop talking about your successful career." Steven's eyes shone with admiration. "Jose is very proud of you."

What in the world had Grandpa told him?

Her grandparents hadn't played matchmaker in nearly a decade, since she'd moved to Colorado Springs for her first teaching job. And this was a lousy day to make up for lost time. She looked as if she'd just come from the mines, with no makeup and stains darkening her clothes by the minute. "Grandfather talks when he's upset."

"I can vouch for that," Steven said with a chuckle. "I enjoyed his company."

"You probably didn't get a word in edgewise." Tori's hand reached for her keys and pulled them out. "Good grief, it's almost lunchtime." As if on cue, her stomach growled again. "While your clothes are washing, we can order lunch. It's no bother." Except that she needed to eat something as soon as possible.

"Much as I'd enjoy that, you have—"

She felt a wave of dizziness and hurried to the elevators.

"You okay?" He pulled her away from the door and pressed the elevator button. "Can I get you anything?"

Would this embarrassment never end? "I'll be fine

as soon as I eat something." She reached into her bag. "I was in such a hurry this morning, I forgot the bagel I toasted. I have hypoglycemia. As my emergency granola bar will prove, I haven't had a problem with it for a long time." She held up the foil pouch with the label worn off, and tore it open, then took a bite.

"I think maybe I'd better drive," he said.

"You've done too much already, Steven."

"Friends call me Steve." The elevators opened and he ushered her inside. A group of female nurses stared at them in silence. "Parking garage, please."

She lifted her gaze to his, "I parked in the east lot."

"We're not taking your car," Steve said.

She shook her head. "You don't know where I live."

"I'm about to find out, because you're in no condition to drive." As if he, too, had become aware of the attention they were drawing, he added, "With the stress of your grandmother's stroke, you have to be sure to eat and take care of yourself."

The elevator stopped and the nurses left, giggles erupting as the doors closed.

"Stroke? She had a stroke?" Tori collapsed against the corner of the tiny cubicle. The air seemed to be getting thicker.

He looked at her, shocked. "Isn't that what they said?"

"I didn't hear that specifically. I didn't want to ask...." She took several deep breaths. "What a spectacle I've made today. I'm not usually like this, Steven."

"Steve." He lifted her chin. "Don't do this to yourself. It's been a lot to handle, with your parents out of the country on a mission and no one else nearby to help. It wouldn't be easy on anyone."

She willed back the tears she wanted desperately to shed. "I'm not ready to let her go. *Abuela* practically raised me."

"The doctor sounded hopeful."

The elevator opened and they stepped into the cool air of the parking garage. "You really think he sounded positive, that she's going to be okay?"

"I do." Steve led the way to his truck. "Of course, you need to be realistic at the same time. She may not make a full recovery. But your grandmother is a strong woman who will get through this."

Tori didn't want to hear platitudes—from the doctor, a nurse or a good-looking, smooth-talking rancher who had probably never met her grandmother before. "*Abuela* is strong, and she won't give up. I won't let her."

Steve opened the passenger-side door and helped her inside. "I don't doubt it for a minute."

She poured some of the broken granola into her mouth and crunched so loud she couldn't hear herself think. "So what do you want for lunch? There are several fast-food places to choose from between here and my place."

"I'd just as soon get you home. We can grab a bite there. You need to get back to your grandparents."

She gave him the once-over. "You don't look like the yogurt-and-fruit kind of guy—" Her door closed, cutting her off. Watching his confident stride take him around the truck, she felt like a teenager ogling a new kid at school. He opened the driver's door and stepped up. "And that's about all that's in my fridge at the moment."

"You're right about that, but I can get something to eat when I run errands." He started the truck and backed out, then gave her a choice of right or left when he reached the exit of the parking garage.

Tori pointed to the right.

"I'm very curious just what kind of guy you think I am."

"Haven't met a rancher yet who would turn down any sort of beef. Besides, that fruit and yogurt just didn't look right on you. Turn left at the next light."

He laughed. "You don't say. So what would a man use to figure out what sort of woman you are?" He stopped at the red arrow and turned to her. One corner of his mouth lifted in a smile.

Before she could answer, the light changed and she had to give the final directions to her condo.

He pulled into the driveway and opened his door, then reached across the seat and took her briefcase. "Come out this side so the sprinkler doesn't soak you to the skin." Steve offered a hand as she slid across the seat and helped her maintain her balance on the way down to the ground.

"So, what'll it be, Tori? Give me a chance to figure out what sort of woman you are."

Tori felt herself blush. She hurried to put the key in the lock and stepped into the cool living room.

Was he flirting with her? Tori felt an odd sense of regret. One, that it had been so long since she'd had a man in her life that she had to stop and assess their conversation to answer her own question. And two, that she hadn't even realized until just now exactly how long it had been since she'd been out on a date.

Whatever the case, she shrugged, unable to even think of one answer to his question. "If I'm going to wash our clothes, we're going to have to take them off first."

Chapter Two

"I don't believe I just said that!" Tori's neatly manicured hand covered her face as she blushed a deeper shade of pink. "I didn't mean that the way it sounded."

Steve laughed. "That tells a lot about what kind of woman you are. It's quite revealing." He took the hospital scrubs from her clutches. Her thin face and high cheekbones glowed pink clear down to the V of her polo shirt. "And you thought you needed to eat. Looks like all you needed was someone to get your heart pounding again."

Long, delicate fingers inched down her cheeks and those onyx eyes looked up at him. He could drown in her gaze.

Wished he could, anyway. "I'm sorry. I couldn't resist giving you a bad time. Which way to the bathroom?"

"First door on the right. I think you'll find everything you need. Towels and washcloths are in the cabinet. Help yourself. I'll order pizza and salad, if that's okay. I think it will arrive the quickest of anything. What kind do you like?"

"Deep-dish, supreme, everything but the kitchen sink."

Tori grabbed half of a toasted bagel, which lay on a paper towel on the ceramic tile table near the door, and held it up. "See this—I had breakfast made." She spread a little peanut butter on it, then took a small bite and reached for the phone, her pointer finger scanning a list nearby. "Drinks?" Tori punched in the numbers, said yes into the receiver and waited.

"Not when I'm driving."

She tipped her head and gave him a stern look that he was certain had been perfected at school.

"Whatever cola they offer is fine. Do you need help getting up the stairs?" He couldn't remember the last time he had felt so young, so intrigued by a perfect stranger.

Now she was laughing, too. "Positive."

His heart stopped and she recited her name into the phone, as if none of this mattered to her at all. It probably didn't, he realized.

Even though they were both educators, it didn't mean they shared the same interests outside of the classroom. He glanced around the room again, hoping he'd find some clue that they had something else in common. The room wasn't simply neat, it was immaculate. One strike against him. It was more than he could manage to keep up with laundry. The furniture looked as if she'd just taken the plastic wrap off yesterday. There were no dishes in the drainer. None in the sink. Did she really live here?

Steve's gaze roamed to Tori, suddenly aware that she was ordering their lunch. She looked to be at least a decade his junior. Surely such an intelligent and beautiful woman had the pick of the crop when it came to men.

Her cell phone rang, and she reached into her briefcase for it while completing her phone call with the pizza parlor.

Their age difference was like a thorn in his side, reminding him that he was no youngster. He had commitments, and his children's needs were his first priority. He let himself dream, just for a minute, that there could be something between them. Lately it seemed like all the available women were fresh out of high school or looking for someone to take responsibility for her and a few kids. Just because his hair was graying didn't mean he was over the hill. Close, but not quite. He disappeared before the thorn began to fester.

From down the hall he heard her voice and paused. Was she talking to him? "Sorry to bother you at work, Chase. How're you today?"

He shook his head. Steve knew better than to think she had no ties. He closed the door a bit, unable to tune out her wonderful, low voice. "I'm sorry. I need to cancel dinner."

There was a pause, then "I know it's been months since we've met, but Abuela Sandoval had a stroke…."

She paused, as if Chase had interrupted her. "Oh, sorry. *Abuela* is Spanish for grandma."

Steve closed the door and stripped off his clothes. It had been a long morning, till he'd met her. And in little more than an hour, this would all be a memory. A very nice memory. Surely she visited her grandparents. Maybe he could casually suggest they get together next time she came to Segundo. Casual? Right. Thus far, you've been about as subtle as the 4:00 a.m. coal train rumbling through the valley.

After cleaning himself up, he waited in the living room, admiring her decorating taste, even if it was a bit too perfect. Southwest decor had been the rage a few years back. His wife had tried it, but Southwest just didn't fit in their Baltimore suburb home. Here, the subdued colors were natural, blending well with the arched doorways and plastered walls. Out the living room window Tori had a view of the Rocky Mountains—Cheyenne Mountain, to be exact. Off the dining room, a view of desolate and flat plains.

Delicate footsteps sneaked up behind him. "The laundry room is downstairs, Dr. Remington." She pinched the shoulder of the green cotton fabric and tugged lightly. "Scrubs don't flatter many people, but on you the look fits."

"Very funny." He followed her with his bundle of laundry. She wouldn't be teasing him if she knew the drastic measures he had taken to avoid following in his father's medical footsteps.

Tori started the washer, added detergent and stain

lifter, then sprayed her clothing and handed the bottle to him.

Steve sprayed a meager amount of treatment then shoved them in the washer and closed the lid. "Is this anything like meeting at the Laundromat over mismatched socks?"

She laughed. "We're a little old for stale excuses for meeting someone, aren't we?"

"Personally, I'm too old to be playing the field at all. But since you asked…your technique could use some work," he teased.

"It might have helped if you hadn't been standing in the doorway." Her tone was different than when she'd broken her date with Chase.

Velvetier.

She stepped away and smiled.

He stared back in amused silence, wondering if they were really flirting. It had been, what, fifteen years since he'd flirted with anyone. The few arranged dinner dates he'd had recently had been about as personable as having dental work done.

Tori broke away from his gaze. "I need to call the school. It's such a crazy time of year." She lifted the phone that was now clipped to her slim waist and apologized yet again.

"I understand." He followed her up the stairs.

Her conversation was short and to the point, reminding the secretary of another project deadline looming.

The doorbell rang a few minutes after they'd settled

into the overstuffed furniture. "I'll take care of this," he said as she pulled a twenty from her purse.

"This is my treat." She handed him the money, walked into the kitchen and pulled plates from the cabinet. From the refrigerator she pulled an overwhelming selection of salad dressings while he paid and carried the pizza to the table.

"So, how do you like Colorado?"

"What's not to like? It was an adjustment from Maryland at first, but it was just what we needed. After my wife passed away, I needed to slow down and take time to bond with my kids."

"I'm so sorry. How did you end up in Coal Valley?"

"My uncle said he needed help keeping up with the work on the ranch, which turned out to be an excuse to give the kids and I a place to escape from well-meaning grandparents. It's been a good move overall."

"Oh, you're Bill Remington's nephew. It just dawned on me. So you're Brody's cousin...."

She sounded as if that changed everything. She looked much younger than Brody, but maybe... "Did you go to school with him?"

Tori had just taken a bite of pizza, so simply nodded. When she finished her bite, she didn't expand on her answer. Had there been something between them?

"That's convenient. Brody's on the school board, and you're teaching there."

A string of cheese snapped, plastering itself to his chin. Tori smiled as he twirled the end around his finger and put it into his mouth. He swiped the oil spot with the back of his hand a second before she produced a napkin.

"It has its good and bad points. I always wanted to teach, but my parents somehow convinced me that I could never support a wife and family on a teacher's income."

"There is some truth to that. Most teachers' spouses are forced to work in today's economy, but it's come a long way in the past few years. Still, if one is looking for country-club status on a teacher's salary, they're bound for disappointment."

"I grew up in the country club and couldn't run far enough away from that life. So far in fact, that I joined the army, got my college degree and didn't retire until two years ago."

"The army?"

"Corps of Engineers."

"So you're teaching with an emergency license."

Did he hear a disapproving edge in her words? He nodded. "When the upper-level math teacher quit mid-year, Brody suggested I give it a shot. I subbed last spring, passed the state licensing test and enjoyed education so much I decided to get my principal's license. I hope to finish next spring with my master's in Ed Leadership. Figure I can help more kids that way."

"I'm impressed." They discussed teaching until the bong of Grandfather's hand-crafted mantel clock reminded her that she needed to get back to the hospital.

"Excuse me while I put your clothes in the dryer." She wasn't more than a minute, yet he missed their conversation.

When she returned, the subject progressed to her upcoming challenge to convince her grandparents it was time to move closer so she could help. "With my parents out of the country, my nearest aunt and uncle in California, my brother and his family in eastern Texas, that leaves me with the majority of the caregiving responsibility. *Abuelo* is stubborn as a mule. I just can't see him willingly leaving his house."

"Surely there's a home health-care network in the area."

"I'll look into it, but I'd feel a lot better if they would move here. With my job, I just don't have much time available to run back and forth. And their house isn't set up well for handicapped living."

Steve smiled, mostly to himself. Jose had mentioned his determination to stay in their home, but he wouldn't tell her that. She already knew the battle ahead of her. "As I'm sure you're aware, the Segundo school district is struggling. I'm sure they would love to have—"

She held up her hand. "I'm *not* moving back to Segundo. It's out of the question."

He took a long swig of soda, hoping to cool his temper before he spoke. "Sometimes we have to look beyond what we want to what's best for those involved."

Tori looked at him, astonished. "How old are your kids?"

Steve felt pride just thinking of his daring duo. "Six and ten. Kyle and Kelsey. I take it you didn't like growing up there?"

"I didn't say that." She shook her head and looked at her salad.

"I believe it was your tone of voice." He took a bite, waiting for her to say what she was really thinking. "So what is it? Why won't you consider moving back if you're the only one who could help your grandparents?"

"Making decisions for your children is your responsibility, Steve. How can you compare that to...?" She stood and started clearing the dishes.

"Compare to what?"

She turned her head and stared at him. "Caring for grandparents is different than caring for your own children. There's so little for my grandparents to do in Segundo. Colorado Springs has better health care, wonderful retirement living facilities and so much more to offer them. I've tried to get them to move, but they won't."

He joined her in the kitchen. "It sounds like your grandfather isn't the only stubborn one in the family."

"I came by it honestly. I have very good reasons for needing them to come here."

"I'm sure you do."

She placed a hand on her hip. "My career can't just be ignored. And let's just say that my education philosophies don't mesh with Superintendent Waterman's."

"You might be surprised. I think things are on the verge of some big changes in Segundo."

"So I've heard."

"What changes would you make, theoretically?"

"I don't live there, so I should stay out of it."

"I asked your opinion. I have a feeling you know something I should know. I'd like to hear your take on the situation."

"Everyone in the valley should be concerned. Parents more than anyone. Teachers need to try more innovative teaching methods. With certain staff still at the school, I know change is an uphill battle. But this isn't about what's easy, it's about what's best for the kids. Surely as a teacher, you're aware of the problems that the schools are facing with test scores."

"I am." Steve leaned a hip against the countertop, mesmerized by her dramatic outpouring. "That's why I agreed to fill the part-time opening. I'd like to be part of the solution."

Her passion to help the students succeed bubbled from deep within her and he admired her determination to do what was best for the kids. Why, then, couldn't she be more objective with her grandparents? A smile crept across his lips.

Tori looked at him accusingly. "What?"

He snapped to attention, erasing the smile as if he'd been a guilty kid caught in the middle of a lie. "I'm just listening. I couldn't agree more. The teachers started working with a literacy coach this summer."

"That's a good start." She turned to the dishwater then pulled out a cloth and started wiping the counters.

She seemed skeptical that Coal Valley Secondary School could meet state standards without major changes. If they couldn't, rumors were that the state would take over and start with an all-new staff.

The thought of the state running the school sent chills up his spine. Maybe he was in way over his head, thinking he could make a difference. After his administrative internship he hoped to find a principal position. If nothing came of that plan though, he would be content to be in the classroom, working with kids full-time. He would do anything to prove to his father that his dreams hadn't been in vain. Listening to Tori renewed his determination.

"I'd like to hear more of your ideas. Since I'm new to education, I have a lot to learn. Maybe we could have lunch sometime."

"I have no idea what my schedule will be like from here on out, but I love talking about education—too much, in some people's opinion." She stared at him. "I hope your year goes well. There's always work for an enthusiastic teacher." Tori slipped the pizza into a plastic bag and offered it to him. At the same time she called the hospital.

While she talked, Steve went downstairs to check on his clothes. They were almost dry, which would do him just fine. She needed to get back to the hospital.

A few minutes later Tori joined him in the basement. "How are things going?"

"*Abuela* is sleeping again and the doctors are still reading her tests." Tori looked understandably impatient. "How is your laundry coming along?"

"Fine. Why don't you get ready, and I'll change.

And don't let me forget to bring your grandfather's suitcase in before we leave."

As if reality had just hit, tears wet her dark eyes. "I wonder how long they'll be here. Not that I mind the company, but it's a very busy time of the year. I don't know what to do."

Steve patted her shoulder. "Take it one day at a time. That's all you can do."

Tori took a deep breath, wiping the tears away, as if determined to regain control. "I suppose you're right." She hesitated, then headed for the stairs. "I'll be ready in a few minutes."

She looked at him approvingly when he walked into the living room a few minutes later. "No stains. I'm glad *Abuelo* insisted we launder them right away. I can't thank you enough for bringing him, and helping me through the day…and not holding it against me when I made an absolute fool of myself."

"God doesn't make fools." He pushed a stray hair away from her eyes. He'd wanted to touch her silky black hair all day. "I hope that when you're in the valley, you'll give me a call. I'd be happy to reciprocate on lunch."

"I can see it now—lunch at the diner. You must like to set the rumor mill a turnin'." She smiled.

Steve felt a twinge in his chest. "I'm sure I can come up with something a little more promising than the diner. Maybe we could take a picnic up the hill and watch the sun set over the Spanish Peaks."

"Hmm. That does sound promising."

Chapter Three

Two weeks later, Tori drove up to the tiny house on Piñon Lane. Unexpected emotions wrapped themselves around her like a cobweb. She stepped out of the SUV, stunned by the dreariness of her grandparents' home. The August heat had sucked the life out of their yard. She touched the lilac bush and the leaves crumbled like crisp tortilla chips. Chrysanthemums drooped over, their bright buds withered. Marigolds and zinnias were dried clusters on the end of gray-green sticks.

It had only been four months since her parents left for the mission in South America, and Tori had been here just weeks before *Abuela*'s stroke. What had happened?

She unlocked the front door and stepped inside. A sour stench permeated the air. Tori hurried from window to window, wrestling them open. *Abuela* had always kept a tidy house, but now clutter filled every table and chair. Dirty dishes were piled in the sink.

Trash hadn't gone out in weeks. How had everything fallen into such disarray so quickly? Why hadn't they told her they needed help? Had she overlooked the signs?

Tori collected the odor-causing garbage, sprayed room freshener and set the trash bag outside the back door. She studied the back entrance, wondering if it might be easier to fit with a ramp than the front. She walked around the house, noticing things looked much different through the eyes of the caregiver. The three steps out front seemed like nothing until she considered how to get *Abuela*'s wheelchair up them and into the house. The wrought-iron handrail wobbled in the slight breeze. It, too, had fallen into a sad state of neglect. The once-neat house looked as worn-out as the owners.

School bells rang across the street and Tori turned, expecting to see the kids run anxiously out of the building, yet not a student appeared. Her alma mater, like the rest of her hometown, looked older, smaller and more withered as a result of the harsh elements and sparse budget.

"Tori!" She heard Steve holler from the school parking lot across the street. He waved, sauntering closer, speeding up with each step. She waved, recalling Steve's occasional telephone calls to check on Grandma's condition. "How are you?"

"Fine," she said, stretching the truth. "I came to see about renovations. They're sending *Abuela* home soon." Tori felt an odd sense of panic. Suddenly taking care of two other people seemed overwhelming. She, who worked seventeen-hour days, was actually feeling out of her realm.

"Why didn't you tell me you were coming? I'd have—"

"It was a last-minute decision. I dropped *Abuelo* off at the care center to spend the day with Grandmother. My brother will pick him up this afternoon. They tried to talk me out of coming here by insisting that it would only take a little rearranging of furniture to make it work."

"I'm sure it won't be too difficult."

Tori appreciated his cheerleading efforts, but he hadn't seen the mess inside. "I'm glad I didn't put this off any longer." She took a deep breath and lifted her shoulders. "I met with the physical therapist yesterday to find out what needed to be done before they could send *Abuela* home. She's paralyzed on one side." Tori shook her head, the weight of the situation winning again. "I just don't know if this is going to work. The rooms are small, doorways narrow and the house is so cluttered." She looked around the yard and felt tears cloud her vision. "This is so unlike my grandparents."

"I came over last week and tried to see if he had a mower in the garage, but it's locked. How long are you staying?"

"For the weekend. My brother and his family are on their way from Texas." She looked at her watch. "Should be arriving any time. He's going to stay at my condo with *Abuelo*...."

Steve looked puzzled. "And you're here to work all weekend? Alone? Have you forgotten it's supposed to be a holiday?"

She felt her eyes flutter closed, pushing the tears down her cheeks. "After two weeks of my grandfather at my house, being alone will feel like a vacation, even if I'm cleaning." Tori closed her eyes. "I'm sorry. I shouldn't complain. I'm just not used to having extended houseguests."

Tori opened the hatch of her SUV and pulled out a stack of empty boxes. Steve got the other stack and followed her into the house.

"Is everything okay at work?"

"The principal suggests I take a few weeks of family leave. How can I even consider taking time off in September?"

"I'm sure they could manage."

She looked at him suspiciously. He seemed awfully agreeable to the idea. "Better than I can, probably. I'm not accustomed to anything but a win-win situation, and this one has none. *Abuela* and *Abuelo* obviously can't take care of each other anymore, but they insist on coming home. Run-down as it is, it's been their home for over fifty years, and they refused to leave 'until God moves them to the castle in the sky,' as *Abuelo* always says."

"Sounds just like your grandfather." Steve laughed and Tori pushed her emotions aside. Now wasn't the time to let down her guard. Especially with someone she hardly knew.

"Yes, it does." She didn't want to feel comforted by his sympathy, his soothing voice or his good looks. She looked nervously around, trying to find some distraction from her weakness for cowboys wearing the mythical white hats. "It was nice of you to stop by, Steve, but I need to take care of some things before everyone is closed for the holiday," she said absently as she rubbed her forehead.

"You're doing great, Tori." He took her by the shoulders and smiled. "Don't worry. It'll work out. You have all day to make your calls." He looked around. "And you don't need to look for a contractor. I'd be happy to do any building renovations you may need done."

"How...?"

"It stands to reason that if Mrs. Sandoval is coming home in a wheelchair that you'd need a few changes to be made. When are they looking at releasing her?"

She hesitated, unsettled by his nearness. "She's making such good progress they keep moving the date up. I don't see how we can be ready now that I know what state the house is in." She knew what teachers' hours involved, not to mention that she wanted to be sure the work was done right, by a professional. "I appreciate the offer, Steve, but I couldn't take you away from your kids and job. And I refuse to take your time on a holiday weekend."

"Maybe we could work out a compromise. I'll see what needs to be done, and you let us take you away from here Sunday afternoon. Aunt Elaine and Uncle

Bill are having their annual Labor Day picnic." His plea was gentle, open for discussion and terribly tempting.

Tori wanted to keep her visit to Segundo as quiet as possible. "I haven't been to the ranch since Brody and I were in high school. I'm not so sure that's a good idea."

"It's nothing too frightening, just the picnic and the annual hayride to end the summer." Steve paused, "Think about it. I pick up the kids around three. Why don't we stop by and mow the grass so you can at least water the trees tonight? You can let me know if we have a deal then."

Tori followed him outside and glanced at the yard. "I'm not sure if I'll be done with my appointments by three."

"If you just leave the garage unlocked, we can get started."

"But I don't even know if the mower is working."

He backed away with a laugh. "I'll see you later. I came out to see if the school bells are working, so I'd better get back."

Tori unlocked the garage then locked the house and slipped into the car to run her errands, surprisingly anxious to see Steve again. She returned long before two o'clock with a few groceries and a very short referral list from the health care coordinator of handymen who had experience with handicap renovations. At the top of the list was none other than Steven Remington. She had called several of the others on the list from her cell phone, but all were busy until the end of the month. While she liked Steve, she wasn't sure it was a good idea to hire him to do the work. He had a job and children, and who knew how much time the building would take?

Tori carried her supplies into the house and removed several containers of green growing things from the refrigerator, replacing them with her own meals for the weekend. By the time Steve and his kids arrived, she'd made room for the box of ice pops in the freezer and met them outside when she carried the trash bag to the garage.

His kids jumped out of the truck and waited for their dad.

"Kyle, Kelsey, this is Miss Sandoval."

"Just Tori, if that's okay with you. I'll think I'm back at school. How are you kids today?"

Two meek voices murmured, "Fine."

"Hasn't school started yet?"

Kelsey shook her head, but Kyle spoke. "Not until next Tuesday. This is our last weekend of summer vacation."

"Do you have fun plans?" Tori asked.

"We're going on a hayride, and ride horses and maybe even swimming." Kelsey blurted out, "Dad says maybe you could come with us. Will you?"

Tori smiled. She was flattered that his daughter didn't feel threatened by sharing her dad's attention. "I'd like that, but I do have a lot of work to do here."

"Bummer." Kyle looked up to his dad and frowned.

Seeing that the kids' disappointment matched

Steve's surprised her. She presumed that Steve had told his kids that he had offered their help during their last weekend of the summer vacation. "I'll see how much I get done. How about that?"

Their faces brightened.

"Sounds fair enough." Steve clapped his hands once. "Let's find that lawn mower and get to work."

Tori led the way to the backyard and the kids took off when they found the rickety old swing set that her grandfather had built from discarded supplies from the mine.

The kids stood examining the structure, tugging on it before climbing aboard. "Dad, I'm going to get your tools from the truck, okay?"

"Sounds good, Kyle. It's unlocked." Kyle disappeared with Kelsey close behind.

"I appreciate your help, Steve, but I don't want you to…"

Steve paused before going into the garage. "I'm not going to take anything away from my family," he whispered. "It's important that they learn to help others, and I make sure they are appropriately rewarded for doing so."

Her willpower faltered. Then Steve's mouth twitched and she caved in. "If you're sure."

His immediate smile told her that there wasn't much Steve Remington wasn't sure about—even the humbling experience of raising children by himself. "I am. Did you have any luck arranging for home health care?"

She felt the insecurity creeping back. In the city, care for the aging was a hot commodity, but here it had always been a family responsibility. That meant her. "They're overbooked and short-staffed. They can't offer much more than once-a-week service. I'm going to have to find someone who isn't part of the home-health system to come and help."

"Did they have names of qualified people?" While they talked, she and Steve unburied the mower.

"A few. I recognized a few names from school, so I'll start there, I guess. They also gave me a list of men who could do the renovations."

Steve moved a cast-iron birdbath. "You won't need that list. I'd be insulted if you don't let me do the work for you." Tori set aside a box of old clay pots, along with the special memories they held, choosing to over-look Steve's comment for the moment. It was almost tradition for households to include several generations in the valley. And surprisingly, that crossed all cultures and social classes. Even the Remingtons, with all of their money, kept family on the ranch. She looked at Steve with an unusual jealousy. While he'd left the cir-cle of his own parents, he'd still come back to family for solace. Her family broke every cultural boundary for the times.

Steve pulled the mower into the yard where they could take a better look. He yanked on the cord and nothing happened. "Sounds pretty dead." Rubbing his chin, he stood and moved the mower closer to his toolbox.

Tori forced her unruly emotions to the back of her mind, focusing on the present. "Steve, you're going to ruin your clothes. This doesn't have to be done today."

"I don't suppose you have those scrubs around, do you?" His eyes twinkled, and she was convinced that he wanted to say something more.

"I returned those to the hospital," she said, reading way too much into his gaze. "I'm sure I could find something, though it wouldn't look nearly as cute on you." Why did she suspect that they would be having a much different conversation without the kids here?

He laughed. "I think I have my basketball clothes in the truck. Probably wouldn't be a bad idea to change. I'd hate to have you indebted to me again."

Tori rolled her eyes. "Oh, really? Maybe I should ask for a written estimate before you start the renovations. Not sure I can afford your help."

"It shouldn't be a problem."

She didn't want charity, but she would save that argument for another time. "Help yourself to the house. I'll see how the kids are doing."

Steve lowered his already deep voice, imitating Arnold Schwarzenegger. "I'll be back."

Kelsey tossed a twig at Steve. "You're such a dork, Dad."

"King Dork to you, princess." He turned and disappeared.

Tori found herself studying the closeness between Steve and his kids, pleased to discover what a good relationship he'd developed with them. She admired a parent with determination to keep in touch with their children. Not in a monthly letter way like Tori had experienced. Times were different, she tried to tell herself. In her parents' thinking, they'd done nothing wrong. Leaving grandparents to raise the kids was perfectly acceptable in their world, yet Tori had wanted more. And she still longed for the kind of closeness Steve was creating with his son and daughter.

"Tori, which one is a crescent wrench?" Kelsey asked quietly, tugging her from her trance.

Tori dug through the toolbox. "This one," she whispered.

Kelsey handed the wrench to her younger brother and smiled back to Tori.

"Hey, how'd you know which one I needed?" Kyle studied it a minute and smiled. "Thanks, sis." Kyle worked on one side of the toolbox, Steve on the other. An hour later the kids were enjoying the same swing set that Tori had used as a kid, and Steve had the mower cutting grass. She went inside and cleaned until she heard the mower stop.

"Could I fix dinner for your help?"

"Thanks, but I think Aunt Elaine is expecting us for supper at six-thirty."

"Would an ice pop ruin their appetites?" Tori raised her eyebrows and waited for Steve to protest.

He surprised her by accepting the treat. "Since it's a half-hour drive, I think we'll be fine. I'm sure they've worked up an appetite since snacks at Mrs. Niccolo's."

"Bette is watching kids? We were best friends growing up, but I haven't talked to her in a few years. I thought she got a teaching degree."

"She did. She likes child care better, and it lets her stay home with her family. She's the only licensed provider in the valley, and the kids love her." Steve called the kids. Kyle came dragging the toolbox back to the truck. "Here, let me put that away, Kyle."

"Thanks for letting us play on the swing set, Tori. It's awesome. We can swing *really* high on it." Kelsey hugged Tori, surprising her once again.

"Come on in and wash." Tori waited in the kitchen, glad that she had thought of buying refreshments for them. "I have a treat to thank you for your hard work."

"Tori, while Dad works on the ramp tomorrow, could we paint the swing set?"

She was caught off guard. "Tomorrow?"

Steve swallowed a chunk of the frozen confection. "Tomorrow, as in the day after today. You will be here, won't you?"

She nodded blankly. "Sure. I'll see if I can find—"

"We have some leftover paint out at the ranch. If you don't mind multicolors, I think we'd have it taken care of and use up some scraps while we're at it."

She smiled, trying to recall the original color. "That sounds great." She hadn't planned to fix that up, but it would be nice to have the bright colors in the yard again.

The kids devoured the red, white and blue ice pop and begged their dad to let them have another.

"We need to save one for tomorrow. Let's get going

before Aunt Elaine scalps us for being late." Steve looked into Tori's eyes. "We'll see you tomorrow, then."

Steve and the kids arrived the next morning and started working without even ringing the doorbell to announce their arrival. Tori stepped over the piles of magazines she'd sorted through and went outside to greet them. "Morning."

He studied her a moment before saying anything. "I hope we didn't wake you."

She must have looked as bad as she felt. "I fell asleep drawing diagrams of the rooms. I'm trying to rearrange on paper so it's less work. Then I woke at three and couldn't sleep anymore, so I finally just started moving things around. If you have a minute to spare I could use help moving a few pieces into the shed."

He glanced past her into the living room. "You sure that's all you need moved?"

She was getting comfortable with the sound of his voice, a deep baritone that seemed to ease her tension and make everything okay. "Now that you mention it, the curio would work better on the other wall."

Tori expected his smile, almost welcomed it, realizing that, now she was thirty-four, his age mattered less to her than it would have ten years ago. The smile didn't disappoint, but this time, he added a wink as he walked past her.

He inhaled deeply, noting a sweet and spicy scent

pervaded the room. "I think you're right," he said. He pulled out his measuring tape and compared the numbers with the space Tori had saved for it. He shoved the chair a few inches to one side then helped her move the antique cabinet. "There you go. You can put the knick-knacks back inside."

She had washed all of the contents and polished the silver frame of her grandparents' wedding portrait. Steve picked up a smaller frame with Tori's first grade school photo inside. "No question who this adorable little girl is."

"Those were the days," she mumbled.

"And not much has changed."

Tori felt her tired expression melt into a rosy blush and took the frame from his grasp, returning it to the empty shelf. "So what do you have planned today?"

"I hoped to take measurements for the doorways and draw up the plans for the ramp. The kids can't wait to paint the swing set. I hope you really don't mind, and that your grandparents won't, either."

She set her cup of tea on the counter. "I'm sure they would love it. I think they've about lost hope for another generation to use it. My brother's kids rarely come, and as you can see, it's been in such bad condition…."

"Then maybe we'd better get it back into shape, just in case…."

She froze. Surely he didn't mean what she thought he did. "In case?"

"Kids come into your life," he said with a mischievous laugh.

Tori heard Kyle and Kelsey in the backyard and glanced outside. The kids were attempting to spread a canvas drop cloth beneath the swing set. She shook her head. "It's a lost cause."

Steve's voice was a little awkward. "Nothing is a lost cause."

She looked at him in disbelief.

"You shouldn't give up on your dreams, Tori."

"I'm not. I'm just being realistic. I left here simply because I didn't want to end up single and pregnant, living in fear of the mine closing like so many of my friends. I was determined I wouldn't get stuck here, just another statistic...."

"I understand. And for the record, I enjoy father-hood more than anything. If the right woman comes along, I'd have no qualms about having another child, maybe even two."

Tori chuckled. "Thanks for clarifying. Not that it's any of my business, but it's...something to think about." She didn't dare admit that she admired him enough to actually remember the information, even though the one factor that would eliminate any hope for a relationship between them still existed. He loved Coal Valley, and she couldn't wait to leave.

Chapter Four

Steve hadn't been sure what to expect when the family saw his guest at the Stonewall Ranch barbecue Sunday afternoon. They knew he'd taken Tori's grandfather to the hospital, but even he wasn't certain what to make of his and Tori's friendship. One thing for sure was that her presence would get tongues wagging.

Tori pulled her SUV to a stop and waited for several minutes before climbing out. Despite his suspicions that no one would recognize her after all of these years, his cousin Brody did immediately. "Victoria Sandoval." Brody's lingering gaze fueled Steve's suspicion that they had indeed been close friends.

She stared like a frightened kitten into the crowd. Uncertain whether she was looking for him or other familiar faces, Steve watched and waited.

"She's still the finest-looking filly in sight," Brody mumbled. "You didn't tell us you're dating someone, let alone that it's Tori."

Steve raised a brow. "We're not dating."

Brody's smile said he didn't believe it. "We all think it's high time you move on with your life, Steve. Surely Anna would want the kids to have a mother. And from what you've told us about her, she and Tori would have been good friends."

Steve didn't much appreciate anyone reminding him of the similarities between his workaholic wife and Tori. "We're not dating," he said again, then added a test of his own theory that Brody and Tori had once dated. "And I'm not sure *your* date would appreciate you drooling over an old flame."

"Once burned is enough for me, but it didn't damage my eyesight." Brody turned away, nodding to the redhead sitting next to the pool. "Just one word of warning, Steve. Tori's dreams never included Coal Valley, and they never will."

Tori had made that very clear, and he didn't need any more reminders. Tori had pulled her silky long hair into a ponytail at the nape of her neck. The white blouse was plain and yet, on her, the simplicity looked elegant. He sauntered toward her, welcomed by a smile when she caught sight of him. "Afternoon," Steve said softly. "You looked wary for a minute there."

Tori gazed up at the vertical stone formation for which the ranch had been named. "Just overwhelmed by old memories."

"You sure that's all?"

Her smile faded to a guilt-ridden grin. "It's been a long time since I've been here. I was highly tempted to head back to my grandparents' house before anyone saw me."

Tori's sudden insecurity intrigued him. If she didn't want to see everyone, why had she agreed to come? He wanted more than anything to believe her reason included him, but he wouldn't take that for granted, either. "Before you change your mind, why not say hello." Steve touched his hand to the small of her back, encouraging her to join the festivities, offering his support the best he knew how.

Tori pulled away from him as they walked through the opening in the split-rail fence of the parking area, and it became apparent that guests were recognizing her. He eased her toward the beverage tables on the bunkhouse veranda. "Why don't we start out with something to drink," he suggested. "What would you like?"

"I'll stick with some of Elaine's famous lemonade, if it's still on the menu."

"Tradition lives forever here. You sure that's all you want?"

Tori nodded. "Thanks."

Steve poured Tori a glass while his aunt and uncle greeted Tori warmly, expressing their concern and offering a helping hand if needed.

"Thank you. I can't believe how much Steve and the kids and I accomplished this weekend. I couldn't have done half of it by myself. At this rate, we might be ready, after all."

"How's Maria doing?" Elaine asked.

The mention of her grandmother seemed to ease her tension. "She's doing much better than expected. Therapists are hopeful she'll be released within the week."

"That's wonderful!" Elaine said, reminding Tori to keep in touch.

"But you don't have help arranged for her yet, do you?" Steve asked.

She shook her head. "I'll bring *Abuela* to my condo until we're confident she can manage at home. That will give me a little more time to find help here."

"Tori!" Kelsey yelled as she ran across the yard. "I was watching for you."

"From Lookout Point, right?" Tori queried.

Kelsey turned white. "How'd you know?"

"Brody and I were friends a long, long time ago. My grandmother worked here, and when I was old enough, I was a housekeeper for the guest ranch."

Kelsey looked to her father for verification while Tori continued to talk. "It was my very first summer job. And after I finished work, Elaine let me go swimming. That was the best part."

Steve noticed that Tori omitted mention of who had shown her Lookout Point and wondered if that was intentional.

"I love the pool, too!" Kelsey said. "Daddy takes us swimming every day. Well, almost every day. They're draining it next week."

Tori patted Kelsey's shoulder sympathetically. "It's that time of year. Summer is over, school is starting and the travelers don't need a pool to cool off. Not only that. Who wants to clean all of the leaves out of it?" Tori scrunched her nose. "Ooh, ick."

Kelsey giggled. "I like using the skimmer. And I learned how to dive this year."

"Good for you."

Kelsey hadn't left Tori alone all weekend, yet Tori never seemed to tire of his daughter's incessant need to talk. Steve noted Kelsey's mood had improved greatly since she'd snagged Tori's attention. Why was it so different than having Aunt Elaine around for that female companionship? he wondered.

"What's your favorite thing about starting school in the fall?" Tori's enthusiasm showed how much she loved her job, but when Kelsey didn't answer right away, Tori added, "Are you anxious to see all of your friends again? Do you like choir, or maybe it's the shopping for new clothes?"

Kelsey shrugged, a smile hiding her ambivalence. "Sort of, I guess. Summer was too short, but school will be fun this year. I have Miss Wilson for a teacher. She's neat."

"Sorry to interrupt, but where's Kyle?" Steve asked, realizing he hadn't seen him since they left the house.

"He and cousin Matt went to the stables to see the pony."

"I'd better go check on them. Care to join me?" He addressed both of them, but his gaze lingered on Tori's subtle smile.

"Sure. Kelsey, are you coming with us?"

"No, thanks, I'll see if Aunt Elaine needs help." She skipped away toward the commotion.

Tori glanced at Steve. "She's quite a young lady."

"Girl," Steve corrected. "Don't make her grow up, or me get older any quicker than necessary." He laughed. "It's probably more like she doesn't want Kyle to know that she tattled on him."

"Give yourself credit, Steve. She's a special young... ster." Tori kept a yard or two between them as they strolled to the corrals.

"Nice save." Steve chuckled. The silence stretched awkwardly as their shoes collected dust from the tall grass. "So I guess there isn't much of Stonewall Ranch that I could show you, is there?"

Tori's eyes sparkled. "Probably not, but I'm sure it would look just as wonderful after..." She paused. "Almost sixteen years. Ouch. Where did time go?"

"I hate to tell you, but time disappears twice as quickly from here on." He didn't add that it tripled when kids entered the house.

"Now who's painting a picture of aging?" With a smile like Tori's, the years disappeared. Steve hated that she would be going back to the city where her life must seem so rewarding and full. He knew life in Segundo must look dull in comparison.

After saving the pony from the clutches of two young boys, she and Steve escorted the kids back to the gathering where the country band was stirring interest with their skilled fiddling.

Steve motioned for Kelsey and they stepped to the

end of the food line where the young cousins attacked the platters with cowboy enthusiasm. Tori gave up with filling her own plate after greeting old acquaintances and answering incessant queries about her grandparents caused more than one delay in the moving of the line.

She had just gotten back into the line when Superintendent Waterman appeared next to her. "Tori Sandoval. It's good to see you again."

She offered her hand. "You, too," she said, caught very much off guard. Jerry Waterman had looked old all those years ago, when she'd been a student at Coal Valley Secondary School, and time hadn't been kind to him. His tan appeared dull and faded, his eyes sunken and his breathing shallow and labored.

Steve looked concerned. "How are you feeling, Jerry?"

"I can't say in mixed company. That West Nile is a tough nut to crack." He shook his head and caught his breath. "I'm hoping the worst is over. I've tried to reach you at your grandparents' home, Tori, but I keep missing you."

"Really? I just arrived Friday."

"Yes, I noticed your car in the driveway. How is Maria?"

Tori gave him the condensed version of *Abuela*'s rehabilitation and hoped his only intention in calling was to check on her grandmother.

Steve finished filling the kids' plates and settled at the table. Did he know something she didn't?

"Steve tells me you're an administrator now. Of course, your grandparents told me a while back, but I've lost track of time. How do you like it?"

"This is my fourth year, actually. It's quite a change from the classroom, but I enjoy the challenges."

After an awkward mention of the state-mandated student-assessment tests, Tori suspected he'd come out of his way specifically to talk to her about local results. "Why don't we finish serving ourselves and sit down to visit?" she said. At least with the discussion focused on education, Tori felt comfortable and in control. After the direction of the conversation with Steve yesterday, she needed all the help she could get to keep herself focused on her grandparents' care.

Jerry was well-known for his healthy appetite, yet the portions of roasted pork, barbecued ribs and salad he was taking indicated he wasn't as much on the mend as he wanted people to think. "I'm sure you've heard about the problems at Coal Valley," Jerry said as they served themselves from the buffet table.

She wasn't sure if she should admit that she kept her eye on what was happening in her hometown school district or play ignorant. "Colorado Student Assessment scores are always in the news. There isn't a school in the state that isn't scrambling to raise scores in at least one area."

"Oh?" Jerry lifted his bushy eyebrows. "What has your school been working on?"

Tori briefly explained her school's implementation of a literacy program and Jerry's eyes brightened.

"How did it work? We're starting the literacy coaching program this year." They carried their plates to the table where Steve and his kids were seated. Steve excused himself to get drinks, and Tori felt guilty hiding behind the discussion of work.

Jerry quietly voiced his apprehension with the new program. They bounced ideas back and forth, sharing stories of successes and failures of the educational system over the years.

When Steve returned, the "chalk talk" ended abruptly. "I shouldn't be making you talk shop when you're on a date. What am I thinking?" Jerry exclaimed.

"We're not—"

"No need to make excuses," Jerry said breathlessly. "This isn't the time to discuss business, anyway. We'll talk later." Soon afterward, Uncle Bill started hayrides and Jerry stood to leave. "Tori, it was good to visit, but I'm plumb tuckered out. I'll be in touch."

His sudden departure puzzled her, but she supposed he tired easily after his battle with the virus. "I'd be glad to offer any help I can, Dr. Waterman." She was surprised by her desire to help and the determination to follow through with her promise. She worried about Jerry's health.

She visited with more old friends and schoolmates while they waited for the first group to get back from the hayride. When their turn came, Steve helped her onto the wagon, but Kelsey squeezed herself between her dad and Tori, endearing herself to Tori. Tori knew

Steve was a catch most women wouldn't turn away, but there were too many marks against them. She had enough on her shoulders without adding the pressure of a romance. She simply needed to keep her distance.

Tori had enjoyed seeing old friends again, as well as the beautiful sights of the ranch. She stayed late into the evening, hoping for a chance to speak with Steve alone. After the kids had fallen asleep she realized Steve had misunderstood her reason for staying. He found a movie on cable and tempted her with a bowl of popcorn.

"Steve, we need to talk."

"About?" Steve set two sodas on the coffee table and sat down next to her.

She backed away.

He raised an eyebrow. "I've had the feeling all day that something's been bothering you. What is it?"

She nodded, deciding to keep the discussion as far from her personal feelings as possible. "I had the distinct feeling Jerry's visit to the barbecue was carefully orchestrated."

"And why do you think that?" he said with a hint of annoyance.

She folded her arms across her chest. "Possibly because he didn't spend a minute with anyone else. He had one purpose, to quiz me about CSAP scores. And he seemed to know just a little too much to have led into the subject by accident."

"And that's my fault? It certainly wasn't my idea to have him captivate your entire day. I'd like a chance at that myself."

She paced the room, afraid to look him in the eye. She couldn't explain why she was so afraid to let herself feel something for Steve, but no matter, he was off-limits. And it was time he understand exactly where she stood on the matter. "What are you trying to do?"

Steve's bronze eyes met hers. "Why do you automatically presume I'm responsible for Jerry's questions? When a school is doing things right, everyone hears about it. So you can't blame me for that. Administrators do keep in touch, you know."

She tilted her head and squared her shoulders. "Funny. He never called me up and asked any questions before you came into the valley. I think there's a connection. What did you tell him?"

Steve closed the distance between them. "I did a little research of my own, then shared my findings with Jerry. What he's chosen to do with the information, I have no idea."

She was irked by his cool response. "What are you talking about?"

"Scores took a huge jump after your school worked with the literacy coaches."

Steve hesitated and Tori quietly waited. A few minutes later, after Steve had eaten a few handfuls of popcorn, she said, "And?"

"Jerry's going to be out of the building more than he'll be in…."

She raised her hand to stop him. She forced her voice lower, choking the words out slowly and precisely. "Not going to happen. I don't belong here anymore."

He retained his affability, but there was a critical tone to his voice. "There's a chance you'll be spending more time here, with your grandparents' situation. You know the community, have experience we need and you offered to help."

"From a distance," she snapped impatiently, then shook her head. "I have a job at a school that I love and I'm finishing my doctorate so I can further my career in administration."

"You couldn't do that in a smaller community?"

She shook her head, trying to ignore the hurt in his whiskey-brown gaze. "Not here."

"I didn't say here." He stepped closer and lowered his voice. "I think this issue has a lot deeper roots than you're admitting."

Tori suspected he was right. "That may be true...*Abuela*'s stroke has me a little uprooted, but I know better than to get myself in deeper than I can handle. The mess at the school isn't going to go away by changing one person."

"I didn't mean to make matters worse, but I had to try."

Tori glanced at temptation and turned away. "It's getting late, and I need to leave early in the morning."

The silence widened and the tick of the clock echoed its tormenting melody. Finally Steve caved in and spoke. "I understand about not wanting to see me again, but don't let me chase you away from the fresh air and rest. I can wait until you're gone to work on the renovations."

"I needed a break, but I haven't seen my brother's family in a year. Since we accomplished so much this weekend, I should spend at least one day with them." She rushed to the door and turned, surprised to find Steve following her. "I thought I'd go to my car and get the key to the house for you to finish working. I can get it from you when we get back to town."

"I'll walk you down to the parking lot."

"Oh…" she said. "Okay."

Steve paused. "Let me look in on the kids once more to be sure they're really asleep."

Tori waited for him outside. It was so quiet she could almost hear the aspen leaves drift to the ground. She missed the stillness of the mountain nights—the reminder of a simpler time. "Looks like everyone's turned in for the night," she said when she felt the vibration of his footsteps behind her.

"Even the kids are worn out. I don't think they've moved an inch since their heads hit the pillows. Have you considered requesting an emergency sabbatical to care for your grandparents? You could finish writing your thesis while you're here…."

She ducked under the low branch of the ponderosa pine and kept walking. "I looked into it, and the school board won't consider it with the budget crises. And I won't leave my job. I can't."

"Every day together is a ray of sunshine," Steve said softly. "For you and your grandparents. Your grandfather literally glows when he talks about you."

The stillness stretched tight between them. She had

spent weeks convincing herself that her decision wasn't selfish, it was logical. Someone in the family would need a decent income to pay for the additional expenses. Her parents were on a mission and didn't have much to spare, her aunt had to quit her job when the cancer returned and her brother had a family. "It's not easy for me to see them come back here without help, Steve. I wish I could do more, but I can't."

Steve shook his head.

They reached her SUV and Tori pressed the unlock button on the keyless entry. When she finished digging out the set of house keys, Steve leaned against the back door and looked up. Tori joined him. "I miss stargazing in the city."

"There are lots of things that look clearer in the mountains—not just the stars." He turned to face her and paused as if he was going to ask something. Tori waited, wondering if she was imagining it.

She handed the house keys to him and he wrapped his long fingers around hers. "I won't let you down. Ever."

Tori's heart pounded so hard she could feel the blood pulse in her fingertips.

Steve leaned forward and without a word, gently pressed his lips to hers, muddying her thoughts and convictions even more. Tori's confusion exploded as a quick and disturbing thought came to mind. Surely he didn't have anything to do with the school board's refusing her request for the sabbatical.

"Good night, Tori. Drive carefully." Steve turned

and headed back up the path to his family as Tori tried to clear her mind so she could do just that.

She jerked the door handle so hard that her hand flew off the chrome and took a fingernail with it. "Ouch!" She instinctively popped her finger into her mouth, as if that would help. Only thing it did accomplish was to keep her from waking Steve's aunt and uncle. She climbed into the driver's seat and closed the door firmly behind her, glancing at Steve's silhouette as he approached his cabin.

"I don't care what you do, Steven Remington. I am not coming back to stay!"

As if he'd heard her, he turned and waved.

Chapter Five

Three weeks later, Tori arrived in Segundo with her grandparents and a car full of medical equipment. Her grandmother had managed well at Tori's condo, and now it was time to move home. The house had changed even more since she'd left. Steve had apparently kept the kids busy painting the outside of the house; whether to tempt her into following his advice or simply irritate her, she wasn't sure.

The school bell rang as Tori helped *Abuela* transfer her tiny frame into the wheelchair. "Goodness, it's nice to be home," said *Abuela* with teary eyes. Thanks to the dedicated speech therapist, *Abuela* had recovered her full vocabulary with no problem. "Looks like school started without us, Jose."

"The house and yard look wonderful, Tori," Grandfather added. "You take such good care of us." He ambled up the ramp and unlocked the front door. "Oh, my." He looked at Tori again. "You couldn't have slept a wink when you came over Labor Day. Didn't need to take the name seriously."

Tori pushed *Abuela*'s wheelchair up the ramp and into the living room. "Steve Remington and his kids did most of it. In fact, I think they must have painted the house, too, while I was away. Doesn't it look like it's been freshly painted?"

Maria smiled. "Everything looks so nice, angel."

Tori kissed her grandmother's cheek. "We had to move some furniture into the shed, but when you're walking again, we can move it back," Tori said hopefully.

Abuela sighed. "Those therapists are pulling your leg. I'm paralyzed, and that's not going to change."

Tori hadn't heard her grandmother sound so negative before. "¡*Abuela!* Don't even think such things. I'll work it out to get you to the therapist, don't think you're work's done yet. You remember Mrs. Gordon, don't you? Look how well she walks after her stroke."

She nodded. "I just don't know if I can do it," *Abuela* admitted. "She looked much younger than eighty-something."

"And you look much younger than that, too, so drop the excuses." Tori realized just then that everything she had accepted as status quo had changed with her grandmother's stroke. Tori was now the caregiver, not her grandparents. She softened her voice and her attitude. "I know it's a little frightening, but we'll get through it together." *Don't make promises you can't keep, Tori.*

After her grandparents were settled and she'd un-loaded their bags, Tori went to the local market to pick up a few perishables. Most of the townsfolk did their main shopping in the city at the chain stores, but thanks to the senior citizens, the tiny store thrived.

She'd no sooner stepped inside the store when she overheard the latest local news—Jerry Waterman had suffered a heart attack. After their long discussion at the Stonewall Ranch picnic, Tori knew that meant trouble for the Coal Valley schools. It would be challenging to lose either a principal or a superintendent, but when the same man filled both positions, as Jerry did, this could be dev-astating. She stalled around the corner hoping to find out more about his condition from the local gossip chain.

Tori's ears perked up immediately when she recog-nized the voice speaking belonged to her chemistry teacher, Mrs. Primrose. "He's in intensive care at the Pikes Peak Memorial Hospital," she said, going on in further unpleasant detail. Dr. Waterman's fight with West Nile Virus the past summer had apparently caused the attack.

A gravely voice said, "I don't know how they're going to avoid replacing him. With the school already on the endangered-schools list, the district is going to fold for sure if they don't."

"Don't be ridiculous, Fran," Mrs. Primrose argued.

"I'd hate to see what the state board of education would do with reform. They haven't a clue what our kids need," Fran said with vehemence. "I suppose they'd fire everyone and start over."

"Not necessarily," Mrs. Primrose muttered, as if she didn't want to argue here in public. "Speaking of starting over, I hear that Maria Sandoval is home. Tori brought her and Jose home today."

Tori shook her head, quickly reminded that news traveled at lightning speed in a small town.

"I heard that, too, but I heard the granddaughter is still looking for home health care for Maria," the other woman said. "What a dismal thought that is," she added in a hushed tone.

"If anyone can come up with a solution, it's Victoria. She's a sharp cookie. Straight-A student, you know."

Tori couldn't help but blush. Mrs. Primrose sounded like a proud parent. The kind of parent she'd always wanted for her own.

Setting milk and cheese in her cart, she headed across the market to the meat counter, hoping she wouldn't get caught eavesdropping. She gave the butcher her order then waited, pondering the grim truth about finding help for her grandmother. She'd talked to dozens of people about the part-time job. If the gossip she'd heard could be trusted, it reassured Tori that her instincts had been accurate. They should have stayed in the city. She noticed fall mums sitting outside, and told the checker to add a dozen to her order. Maybe the color would add a little cheer to the household.

The week went on, and Tori became more discouraged. Her hopes of finding a caregiver to help her grandparents dwindled. Though there were many well-meaning offers, those who were qualified to assist a disabled patient had little time available; those who had time didn't have appropriate training or experience, and no guarantee that they would follow through on the friendly offer.

Members of the family called to check on them, but no one extended a hand. Her dad's sister was going through another round of chemotherapy in Texas, her brother and his wife had children in school and her parents couldn't cancel the mission. She was well aware that their hearts were with her, but their hands were with God. "You're in our prayers," they always added as they said goodbye. Tori wasn't sure how much God would do on her behalf, but she hoped He didn't give up on her quite yet.

Tori noticed the pots of unplanted mums begging for attention outside the garage door. The days had been so filled with phone calls and interviews that she'd postponed yard work until it could no longer be ignored.

Though her grandfather assured her that he could take care of the yard, Tori knew how taxing that would be on his own fragile health. She had three weeks of sick leave remaining; she may as well keep busy. Gardening would be a welcome break from her newly acquired title of "caregiver."

She pulled the dead plants and loosened the soil to prepare it for the chrysanthemums. At least they would keep their color through the chilly mountain nights.

Tori dragged the trash cans to the edge of the driveway for pickup the next morning and carried the plants to the front yard.

"Afternoon." Steve sauntered toward her, waving to students as they drove past. "How are you doing?"

Tori loosened the roots then set it into the hole she'd dug and patted the dirt around the plant. "I'm hanging in here." She brushed the dirt from her hands and tucked a lock of hair behind her ear. "And you?" Tori sat on her heels and looked over her shoulder, ignoring the urge to jump to her feet and meet him at the fence.

He shrugged. "Keeping busy." He briefly mentioned the principal's heart attack and the challenges it had created at the school. "I don't suppose you've reconsidered taking a sabbatical, have you?"

"Are you asking personally, or professionally?"

"Both." His lips formed a tentative smile. "I have no say in the professional variable, but I'm not above praying rather selfishly on occasion."

She laughed. "I see. I'll remember that."

"Be sure you do." A car honked behind Steve, and he turned to wave to the car full of teenagers. "Sometimes when a door closes, God opens a window of opportunity."

She didn't much relish the idea of admitting she'd followed his advice, but it would soon be obvious to everyone that Tori was here for an extended stay. "I've put in another appeal for an emergency sabbatical, but it doesn't look too hopeful. And I don't need to hear any more about open windows. My grandparents need me here so my stay has been extended, but it's not permanent." Tori tried to stay focused on the plants.

"I understand. Family comes first." His smug response grated on Tori's nerves, and she turned just in time to see his equally smug smile fade into feigned ambivalence.

Another car horn honked, causing Steve to look at his watch. "I need to get Kelsey to piano lessons. Give your grandparents my best."

"Say hi to the kids for me," Tori said, frustration creeping to the surface as the outline of his athletic physique disappeared around the corner of the school. "Selfish prayers, huh? Maybe I'll try a few of my own," she muttered, ignoring the honk of his pickup as it rumbled past.

Over the next few days problems continued to crop up. The therapist insisted her grandparents' home was too small to allow *Abuela* room for home treatment. If she was going to get therapy, they would have to take her into Trinidad twice a week, yet it was too far for her grandfather to drive even if he could manage the wheelchair and her grandmother.

Tori's calendar had become more complex than she could ever have imagined with doctors' appointments, physical therapy twice a week and occupational therapy every third day. She felt like a soccer mom carting the team from hither to yonder.

The phone call from Kevin, her principal, caught her off guard. "Tori, Jerry Waterman called me yesterday from the hospital."

"You know Jerry?"

"I do now," Kevin said. "He and Nick Pariso came up with an idea that may help solve your situation."

"I didn't know I had a situation." Tori felt her defenses rankle. "For the record, what do Jerry and our superintendent have to discuss?"

"Careful there. At least hear me out."

"This is sounding worse by the minute. I don't have a situation, Kevin. I have grandparents that I'm helping get settled. This doesn't take—"

"How's it going? Have you found help yet?"

Tori wanted to sound optimistic, even though she'd given up the search. She only had another week, before she ran out of leave time, to convince her grandparents to return to Colorado Springs with her until her parents returned to the States. "It's going well," she fibbed. Just a little stretch of the truth. As long as she was around to run interference with catastrophic schedules, things were running smoothly.

"Another mental reservation?" Her boss knew her too well. "I'm sure this idea isn't as bad as you think it is."

"It's sounding like the board turned down my request. Cut to the chase."

"I'm sorry, Tori. They felt it would set a precedent that they couldn't encourage. Our sabbatical policy is meant purely for research and education, not extended sick leave."

She heard the school bell ring in the background and felt a tug on her heart. As much as she missed her job, she knew it would be no easier to leave here, worrying about her grandparents. "So what's your idea?"

"I'm sure you've heard that Jerry won't be returning to work full-time for months…."

"So the rumor mill is pretty accurate, huh?"

"Afraid so. He's suggested that the school board hire a replacement, temporarily, at least."

She knew what was coming. "Don't say—"

"I know how you feel about going home, Tori, but I think you should consider it. We can't approve a sabbatical, and you'll run out of sick leave in another week. If you take a leave of absence, we can hold your position until next fall. Especially if we form a partnership with the Coal Valley schools." Kevin rattled on, explaining their idea of having the two schools work together to mentor one another in areas of school improvement. "With the mentorship, you'll stay in touch with us, and maybe by the time Jerry's able to return to work, hopefully your grandparents will be in a better situation."

Tori felt a lump in her throat. She felt the doors closing, and wanted to run from the opportunities blooming before her. Her knuckles were white from clenching the phone receiver so tight.

"Think of the relief of being able to help your grandparents, of the opportunities for research for your doctoral thesis, not to mention finding love in all the wrong places."

She heard the laughter in his voice and traded her frustration for some good-natured sparring. "I never should have told you about running into Steve at the hospital. Nothing is going to come of it, anyway."

"Life's full of surprises."

Tori heard the buzzer on the oven.

"Victoria, dinner's ready," yelled *Abuela* as if Tori were on the other side of the school yard.

She stepped out of the yard swing and headed inside. "I need to go, Kevin. Don't authorize my leave yet. I really need to think about this."

"Think fast. The president of the school board there is expecting you to meet them tonight at an emergency board meeting. He'll call with the details. According to Jerry Waterman, you're well aware of the urgency to fill his shoes."

"You're feeding me to the wolves."

"You can make this a win-win proposition, Tori. Put your ego aside for a minute and look at the possibilities."

"With all due respect, Kevin, you have no idea what you're asking." They said goodbye and she turned off the portable phone, heading into the house to do what she'd come here to do—take care of her family.

Her grandfather met her at the door. "I wondered if you'd fallen asleep out there."

"With the school yard not fifty yards away?" Tori laughed as she gave him a hug. She followed him into the kitchen and opened the cupboard. "What vegetable should we have today?"

"Can I help with anything?" *Abuela* said from her wheelchair, struggling to get it turned around on the pile carpeting. "Oh, how I miss your hardwood floors about now!"

"That's an easy problem to fix." Tori grabbed the handles and helped her grandmother turn, wishing she could say something to make her grandparents change their minds. "Things went very well at my house."

"We couldn't impose. Besides, this is our home." Grandfather motioned Tori away and helped his wife into the compact kitchen.

Tori worked her way around them both to get the enchiladas from the oven. Grandfather had already set the table in his own unique fashion: silverware in the glass, napkin covering the plate. She set the lettuce and sour cream on the table, along with a dish of carrot sticks.

"Where are the tortillas? And the beans? We always have them with enchiladas."

Tori played ignorant. She'd trimmed the extra fillers from her own diet years ago. "Whoops, I forgot to buy more."

"There should be extra tortillas in the freezer."

"They were dried-up and broken."

Abuela nodded understandingly. "They must have been a year old. I bought them for the family reunion last year."

Tori mentally cringed. Thank goodness she'd thrown them away.

Abuelo recited their traditional blessing, and they finished their supper without further interruption. While doing dishes, the phone rang and she waited for the dreaded announcement that it was for her.

"Victoria?" Grandfather seemed both shocked and disappointed. "Yes, she's here…Brody."

Before he could get out of his chair, Tori reached across the back of the small sofa and pulled the phone into the kitchen with her.

She almost wished Brody would have left it to Kevin to send the message so that she could claim not to have received word to attend the board meeting tonight.

She greeted her ex-boyfriend with a businesslike tone.

"I'll cut to the chase, Tori. I'm sure you're as thrilled with this call as I am to make it."

"That is a fair statement. It's killing you, isn't it?"

"So Kevin Jordan reached you?"

She may as well resign herself to hearing him out. "Yes."

"And he explained the offer?"

"I wouldn't go that far. He made a general recommendation—from one friend to another."

"Why don't we meet before the board meeting to go over the contract?" Brody suggested.

"I haven't said yes yet. And I'm not so sure I'm going to."

"What's standing in the way? Jerry is determined that you're the person for the job. We have a rather sticky situation, as I'm sure comes as no surprise."

"Why do you say that?"

"Hasn't Steve told you about the speculation among the staff?"

Tori looked into the living room at her grandfather visibly straining to hear her conversation.

"Brody, would it work for me to come to the district offices to discuss this with you?" she wasn't sure what to tell her grandparents. If she didn't take the job, they would blame themselves. If she did, they would feel guilty. They didn't need to worry about anything else right now.

"Sure. I'm at the school now. I just met with the staff."

"Is this an awkward time?"

He hesitated. "Why don't you wait a few minutes, let the smoke clear. The board meeting is in the teacher lounge in an hour and a half."

Tori changed clothes, told *Abuela* that Brody needed her opinion, then watched as the last vehicle left the teacher parking lot. She crossed the school yard and met Brody at the main doors.

"So what's going on here?" Tori asked as soon as the door closed behind them.

"As you may expect, there are a couple of teachers who aren't pleased with the board's action on this."

"Which is?"

"We feel that finding an experienced administrator immediately outweighs our obligation to open up the position to all applicants."

"Who are you trying to bypass?"

Brody raised an eyebrow. "Excuse me?"

"I know how the politics of schools work, Brody. Who is it that believes they should be hired in this position?"

He led Tori in to Jerry Waterman's office and offered

her a seat while he took the chair behind the desk before continuing. On the floor next to Brody sat a box half-full of Jerry's personal belongings. "No one that we can consider. The scores for the upper grades are dangerously low. We have to show improvement immediately in order to avoid state intervention."

"I'm afraid someone has given me far too much credit."

Brody was a rancher. Tori wondered how he had ever been elected president of the school board. "Jerry has talked to the superintendent while he's been at the hospital in Colorado Springs. Several board members contacted members of the staff at your current school. We have no question that you are the right person for this job." He carefully picked up a set of Jerry's family pictures and folded the hinged set of frames together. "I know how badly you want to turn this offer down, and in a way, I understand how you feel. Surely you have to see the timing of all these events is oddly coincidental."

"So I keep hearing." Tori stared at the empty desktop, suddenly terrified at the prospect God was setting in front of her. There was something disturbingly tempting in the offer. She'd always wanted her "own" school, implementing her ideas and programs. And Coal Valley Secondary School was desperately in need of new programs.

They discussed salary, job expectations and her grandparents' needs for Tori's intermittent help.

"We understand that your primary reason for being

here is your grandparents, and we're willing to allow you flexibility in your schedule. We have no doubt that you'll still give a hundred and ten percent to your career, despite your responsibilities at home. It helps that Jerry has an intern this year who's holding things together until we can find a replacement. So if your grandparents have an appointment, you could be available to help them, too." Brody rested his elbows on the desk and intertwined his fingers.

It helped immensely that her grandparents lived not even a hundred yards away from the school. If they had an emergency, she could be there almost as quickly as if she were at the house with them. "You're certainly making a convincing argument. Could we walk around the school?"

Brody nodded. "How long has it been since you've seen the inside?"

"Graduation day."

They visited a little about classmates and class reunions that Tori had missed.

"So it wasn't just me that you ran from, huh?"

Tori was a little relieved that he'd opened the subject. She wanted to get the bitterness out of the way. Especially if she was going to be working for him this year. "I wasn't running from either you, or my past. I was afraid that if I didn't leave then, I'd never leave. I didn't want to end up like so many girls, pregnant, living in fear of the mine closing, working on the ranch as a housekeeper for the rest of my life, to be honest." Tori couldn't believe she'd actually said it out loud.

Brody stopped walking. "And you thought… Were you pregnant?"

"No, no, I didn't mean… Oh, no, Brody. I'm sorry. I didn't date anyone else. And you know there was no way for you and me to be pregnant, but it did seem like an epidemic our senior year." Tori crossed her arms in front of her. "No, I—I wanted to be a teacher, and well, here I am."

"And that's why you broke up with me?" He stopped walking and turned toward Tori, a puzzled look on his face.

"I knew your plans included the ranch. There's nothing wrong with it, but I wanted more than that."

"My wife had a career and lived on the ranch."

And she wasn't his wife anymore. But Tori didn't need to remind him of that. She didn't know what had broken their marriage up. And she didn't need to know. "Don't take it personally, Brody. We were young and I needed more time to grow up and find myself." And her own dreams. And just when she thought she'd found them, she ended up back here. "So, if we're through dissecting our past, why don't we talk about education, and if I really am the right person to fill in for Dr. Waterman."

"You would bring the hands-on experience we need. Your district has already been through a lot of the steps we need to take to keep our schools open. This is your alma mater. Don't you even care…?"

"I'd like a formal interview with a complete overview of the entire situation, staff and academics.

If I'm to be the target of internal conflict among the staff, I want to know who, and why you're not taking applicants."

Brody looked at her oddly. "Well, we can probably arrange that, but we aren't fond of the idea of opening the position to applications."

"Why?"

"Usual reasons. There is a certain staff member we'd rather not deal with throughout the typical application process. The board declared Dr. Waterman's absence an emergency and have received authorization to make an appointment. You don't need to worry about him, though. He blows a lot of smoke, but it's not toxic."

Tori laughed. "Same troublemaker as always?"

Brody nodded. "And he's training an heir."

"Two? There aren't more than ten teachers at the secondary level, are there?"

"Jason Hunt isn't a lost case yet. He does what's right for students, but the limitations in such a small school get to him now and then. That's where Fred Esquival comes into the picture."

"Misery loves company."

"That he does. And I'll admit, working with Jason Hunt has helped quiet Esquival's causes. Jason is able to draw out Fred's more productive qualities, which keeps him focused on the kids."

Tori chuckled. Every district seemed to have at least one rebel with a cause. "What's the overall attitude about the necessary changes?"

"Overall, there's a lot of enthusiasm. I think Fred's worried about his retirement. He doesn't want to find another job, with less than five years to go. Once he understands the vast experience you have, and your passion for education, he'll be your best support. Trust me, Tori. You're the right person for this job."

Chapter Six

Steve wasn't totally surprised that Tori called him after her meeting with Brody and the school board. He wasn't sure it was a good idea, but he agreed to talk with her. She'd even been willing to drive clear up to the ranch after the kids were in bed.

The district needed her, and Steve had to put his personal wishes aside. As the principal's intern, there could be nothing personal between them. Yet if he told her that, she might turn down the job. Only thing worse might be if she wanted to talk about them starting their friendship again.

"Have you heard about the board hiring a replacement for the principal's position?" Tori paced the room, adjusting the red-and-tan scarf to drape smoothly over the shoulders of her black knit dress. "My seat belt doesn't like scarves very well."

"It looks fine, and so do you. Sure I've heard the

news. I'm a member of the staff and my cousin is president of the board."

"Does the staff know who has been asked to take the job?"

Steve shook his head. *So far, so good. I'm not even having to stretch the truth.*

Tori paced to the opposite side of the room and heaved an exasperated sigh. "Do you know?"

Steve didn't like obnoxious people, and right now, he really disliked himself. "Since you're here grilling me, I assume it's you?"

Tori studied him as she walked closer, her steps slowing as she pondered his claim. "You didn't know before tonight?"

"I had my suspicions, but no one actually confirmed them." *The truth is stretching mighty thin, Tori. Stop now, while we still have a chance.* "Can I presume you're considering taking the job?"

"Do you think I should?"

"You sure you want my opinion?" he said dryly. *If she knew him better, she'd know that he got cotton mouth every time he tried to lie. Last time had been during his first week of military school. If he could survive that grilling, he could survive anything.*

"Positive," she said without hesitation. "How do you think the staff will take the school board appointing a replacement for Jerry rather than opening it for applications?"

"Most of us realize there isn't time to waste. We're almost a month into school already. There's a lot of fear of just how far the state will go when they take over. There are even rumors that they could close the school, and no one wants that to happen." Steve offered her a drink, making his way to the kitchen for some water.

She shook her head. "I don't understand who starts these rumors or how they make them so believable. They wouldn't close it, just reorganize."

Steve laughed. "It's not so easy to convince teachers of that fact when they're concerned about a paycheck. Or parents who think their child is going to be bussed to a school thirty or more miles away. It's going to be a challenge for whomever takes over, but surely you realize that."

She looked into his eyes. "Do you think I'm the right person for the job?"

Steve had been suggesting this move for two months, since they'd met. He didn't want anything to stand in her way. He took a long drink of water before answering. "Do you really need me to explain it once more?"

Tori shrugged. "It's a little different now, since the picnic."

Steve quirked an eyebrow. "Yes, it is."

"I thought maybe…" she said, her voice fading to silence. Did he see hope in her gaze?

"We could try again?" He shook his head. "Is that the only reason you're moving here?"

Tori's eyes opened wide and her lips parted. She clearly hadn't expected this kind of response. "Of course not, but as long as I'm here…. I know it would be awkward, but you're only part-time. The math and science department chairman will be responsible for your evaluation…so I wouldn't be your supervisor, exactly."

"I really can't help you make this decision, Tori," Steve said. "Whether or not we could consider more than a friendship is a moot point right now. You made me understand that I shouldn't dangle women in front of my kids' hearts like candy, at least not until I'm sure there *is* a relationship."

Tori nodded, a somewhat bewildered look on her face. "Yes, but what about your selfish prayers?"

"They're between me and God, which is a good place for you to turn for help. Maybe He can help you make the right decision about finding your way home."

Her fine, arched eyebrow lifted in surprise. "I haven't been able to make it to church lately," Tori said. "But I'll be sure to mention it to God when I'm there next time."

Her comment puzzled him. Surely she didn't think she had to be in church to talk to God. "Faith has nothing to do with which church service you attend. Faith is taking God with you wherever you go—to a foxhole, a school, the hospital…. Same goes for talking to Him. If you want my opinion, He's been trying to talk to you for several months now. You're just too concerned with where you're going in life to hear what He's trying to tell you about where He wants you."

Disappointment showed in the straight line of her pursed lips and lowered chin, and Steve hated himself for saying what had come instinctively. "I guess I'm talking to the wrong man then, aren't I?" She forced a demure smile. "Sorry I bothered you tonight."

"Don't worry about it. Hope it helps." He watched her lift her chin and turn away. Steve ached to tell her what his heart wanted her to know—that he'd wanted another chance with her. He knew how difficult the coming months would be, working by her side. He wanted her here, but not by default, he wanted her to stay because she wanted to be here with him. He knew her career came second only to her obligation to family, just as it did for most of the residents of Coal Valley. And after what he'd just done, turning her away like he had, he didn't even stand a chance to come third in her life. Tori slammed the door as she left.

"Sometimes a man has to do what's right, no matter how badly it's going to hurt," he whispered.

Tori's grandparents were asleep when she walked past their room. They, too, had insisted this was Tori's decision; they loved having her stay with them, but they'd manage alone if she needed to go back to her job in the city. She slipped quietly into her room and felt the weight on her shoulders. She had until nine Monday morning to make a final decision. Three days seemed like forever right now. How could she have been so wrong about Steve's reaction to her moving home? About his feelings for her? How could she work in the same school with him after humiliating herself by going to his house? At least he hadn't further confused her by kissing her this time. Still, sleep didn't come easily, and she woke before the alarm sounded the next morning.

She met her grandparents at the breakfast table. "How'd the school board meeting go last night?"

"Fine…" she muttered. "I have until Monday morning to give them an answer. If I accept, I meet the staff Monday after school and go to work Tuesday at seven."

"You'll set things straight, angel. Jerry did a fine job his first fifteen years here, but these past five, he just doesn't seem to have what it takes to make the necessary changes."

"Hmmm. Really," she said.

"Sit down and eat. Breakfast is almost ready. Cup of coffee?"

"Sure." She sat down to an already-set table, deciding she must not have set her alarm at all last night. It was nearly nine already.

It didn't take long for *Abuela* to notice Tori's mind was somewhere else. Though they had tried to make conversation while she ate, Tori wasn't very talkative.

"You never eat a first helping of bacon, let alone seconds. What is bothering you, Victoria?"

Abuelo laughed, kissing her forehead as he walked past her to the sink. "Nothing another bite of bacon won't cure."

Tori pushed her plate away as if she'd just poisoned herself. "Oh, *Abuelo*. What are you trying to do to me?"

"Question is, what are you doing to yourself, child?

You can't starve yourself over a job. God Almighty always provides, Victoria. Like this house," he said, going into the story of the mine closing in the mid-fifties. "We had no job, yet the company sold us this house for less than eight hundred dollars, lot included. Even in those days, it was worth ten times that amount."

"You raise the value every time you tell that story, Jose. Why don't you walk to the market and pick up another gallon of milk. Let Tori and I have some girl talk."

Jose rinsed the soap suds off the plate and set it in the drainer, then dried his hands and put on his jacket. "Sounds like a fine idea. Need anything else?"

Tori jotted down a few items and thanked him for running the errand for her. The door closed, and *Abuela* gave Tori that silent invitation that always caused her to open up. "I'm not at all sure I should take this job, *Abuela*. I'm here because you need me, and this will take me away for most of the day."

"You can't spend all day every minute taking care of us, Victoria. You seem convinced that we need help, and I love having you here, but I have to learn to do things for myself sooner or later." She threw her hands into the air. "I haven't lifted a finger to help anyone in over two months. And if you're here, bless your heart, you rush around doing it all."

"That's why I'm here—to take care of you and *Abuelo*," she said.

Abuela sighed. "And I hate to admit that we couldn't

keep up without you, but you're young and smart, and I see you looking at the school every afternoon. I know you miss the children."

She wouldn't admit to her grandmother that it wasn't nearly as much the children on her mind as hoping she'd see Steve. She had really made a mess of things this time. "Not to mention the money would help out. I could lease my condo out...."

"Or maybe you could keep it, and get away from here now and then. See your friends," *Abuela* said. "As much as we'd miss you, it would be unfair of you to give up your privacy completely. And you're not a teenager anymore. Grown men certainly wouldn't want to come here calling on you with a couple of old geezers in the house."

Tori felt her cheeks warm. "Grandmother! I can't believe you said that! I don't need privacy for a gentleman to call on me. If he isn't content to visit us here, he isn't the right man."

"You're a sweetheart, Victoria. And it's long past time for you to find a man and settle down. Goodness, you don't want to be having babies into your forties like I did."

"Maybe God doesn't have babies planned for me. He certainly hasn't brought the right man to my doorstep. Besides, with no children of my own to worry about, I have plenty of time to devote to the hundreds of special kids at the school, and I have you and *Abuelo*."

"I'm going to get stronger, Tori. I hardly need any

help getting up at night now. Even if you stay and take the job, you need your own space. By the grace of God we'll find a house nearby for you to live."

"I don't…" She started to argue, but her grandmother cut her off.

"Not another word. I won't have a woman your age cramped into a small bedroom without any of your own lovely furnishings. If you won't keep your condo to escape to, we'll find you a place of your own. It's the least we can do when God's been so good to provide for all of our needs, right down to a darling granddaughter."

Tori shrugged. "Fine. Whatever makes you happy, *Abuela*." She figured they'd have about as much luck finding her a place to stay as she'd had finding a caregiver for them. "In the meantime, I'm going to run to my condo this afternoon and get a few different outfits, just in case I take the job. I didn't bring but one dress with me." She cleared the rest of the dishes from the table and set them in the sink. "I should be back in time for supper. Don't let *Abuelo* make anything, I'll bring some of those barbecued ribs and coleslaw from that restaurant downtown." Tori heard the back door open and turned to help her grandfather, only to meet Steve instead.

"What are you doing here?" she said accusingly.

He grinned mischievously. "Your grandfather picked up a few more groceries than he planned on, so I gave him a lift home."

"And you just happened to be at the market, from

thirty miles up the canyon? What a coincidence." *Abuelo* walked past Steve and into the kitchen.

Steve's gaze reminded her that she hadn't cleaned up for the day yet. Her hair stuck out all over, her mascara had probably smudged and she wore her ratty chenille robe and comfy fuzzy slippers. "Not quite. I was headed to the Springs for supplies and groceries for the ranch, and saw him leave the store with quite a handful."

Tori eyed him suspiciously. "He went for three items, not three bags of groceries. Thank you for your help."

"Tori's going to Colorado Springs today, as well. Isn't life full of coincidences?" *Abuela* said with a chuckle.

"Would you like a lift?" Steve said graciously, taking his cue from Grandmother.

Tugging on the robe and her hair, Tori shook her head. "No thanks. I need to clean up and fix lunch before I'll be ready to leave. I don't want to delay you."

"No need to worry about lunch," Grandfather argued. "I picked up a few packages of lunch meats and some extra tortillas. You two go and have a nice day of it."

"Maybe another time," Tori insisted. "Steve has errands to run, and I need to work at my condo."

"Moving?" Steve's eyes sparkled with trouble.

"Yes, I believe I am," she said, challenging him. "Temporarily, until Jerry's back on his feet."

"Then you'll probably need a lot more space to

bring things back than in your SUV. I'll have plenty of room left in the back of the pickup."

Tori felt like a puppet on a string. "I have plenty of room in my own car, but I do appreciate your offer," she said, forcing politeness. "I'll be living here, so I won't need much."

"If you hear of any rentals that are opening up soon, though, let us know," Grandmother added. "Tori needs her privacy, too."

Steve stepped out the door, "What about the place down the street? Or is that too close to the school?"

"Tori's moving out?" Grandfather asked. "Why didn't you say so? I'd have stopped and left a deposit as I went to the store. Looks like a nice place. And the moving van is there now."

Abuela's eyes teared over. "God always provides."

"Let's go talk to the renters, Steve. That'll give Tori time to clean up." Steve followed her grandfather out the door.

"I don't need a place of my own. I'll be fine here," she insisted as the men walked out the door, ignoring her.

Tori was ready when Steve and *Abuelo* returned. Her grandfather was so excited about her possible move that Tori couldn't help but realize she wasn't the only one who needed and wanted a little privacy. "Couldn't be more perfect. Close to everywhere you'll need to be. Two bedrooms, nice kitchen…" *Abuelo* went on and on about a house that was only slightly newer than this one.

Steve handed her the keys. "Want to go see it so you know what we need to bring back?"

"Sure," she said, trying to sound enthusiastic. "Why don't we stop on our way out of town?"

"It wouldn't take but a minute to walk down and back. After you get dressed."

Tori spun around and disappeared down the hall. She returned a few minutes later, annoyed to discover Steve had waited for her. "I have a lot more to do now than I thought I did, so we'd better make it quick." Tori grabbed her purse, and kissed her grandparents goodbye. "Don't hesitate to call Mrs. Primrose if you need help. She's close, and offered to help. Take your medicine at noon, and…"

"I know it's hard to believe, Tori, but we'll be just fine." Grandmother reached out her hand and patted Tori's behind.

"And if you need to stay the night at your condo, go ahead. We'll be here when you get back."

Tori forced a smile, blinked the tears away and walked out the door. She felt Steve's hand on her shoulder and turned away. "I'll see you this evening, if you're serious about bringing some of my furniture back for me." She took a step toward her car.

"Tori? Are you okay?"

"I'll be fine, Steve. Just fine. I'll come here, I'll do the job I'm hired to do and I'll leave when my parents return to care for my grandparents."

He followed her to the car door and opened it for her to get inside. "It's okay to be afraid to leave them alone.

It's no different than leaving kids alone for the first time, or telling them goodbye at their first day of kindergarten."

She took a deep breath. "I'm not usually like this. Heavens, I've only been taking care of them full-time for a few weeks."

"Doesn't matter. They're your grandparents."

"They raised me right here in this house. And now…" She took a breath, willing the tears away. "Irony is, I don't want to be here, and they don't really want me here, either." She glanced at the house at the end of the block. "I guess I'd better go talk to the owners before they leave," she said gloomily.

"You all got used to having your own homes and lives and your own way of doing things. It's never easy to move back in with parents or grandparents. And they probably don't want to admit that they need your help," Steve said. "Think of it as a big house, and you're living at the other end."

"I've never seen a house a block long. You'd have to have an intercom system to talk to each other."

"Yep," Steve said in a hushed tone. "That's how it is."

Tori remembered Steve's wealthy family for whom intercoms did exist. "I'm sorry, Steve. I wasn't thinking."

"It's okay," he said.

"It's not okay. I'm sorry I'm so selfish, but I don't mean to be. I just don't have much experience with…this…." she let the words fade away, trying to think of a way to explain herself. "With thinking of others, sharing, taking care of others. I'd make a terrible mother."

Steve laughed. "That was an interesting segue." He tilted his head. "Someday, maybe I'll show you a house where you do need an intercom to talk to each other. But only for a short visit, kinda like you'd tour a museum."

"I didn't mean any of that in relation to you, or us, or… You made yourself very clear last night. And since we're going to be working together, I think it's wise to keep our distance." She raised her eyes to find him staring at her, comforted to discover that she hadn't been wrong about his feelings for her. "Do you remember how to get to my place?"

He nodded. "Dinner?"

"We can order pizza."

Steve smiled. "Drive carefully."

"I won't be far behind you, and you have my cell number, if you need it, right?"

"I do. You want mine?"

She reached into her bag to find her phone. "I've never seen you with a cell phone."

"I don't have service up the canyon, anyway, but I keep one for when I'm on the road so Aunt Elaine or Bette can reach me." He took a pen from his shirt pocket.

She pulled her cell phone from her bag. "I'll just enter it into my phone. I may need it later on, anyway."

He looked at her as if she'd caught him at something. "The number's 555-5147. See you later."

Tori stopped to look at the house, pleasantly surprised with the condition. The carpets looked new and the kitchen and bathroom had been updated recently. "We fixed it up and tried to sell it, but with our new house finished now, we have to rent it out," the woman explained. "I just put the For Rent sign out this morning. We don't want any pets, but kids are okay."

"Not a problem," Tori said. "I don't have either. And you don't mind if I start moving things in this weekend?"

"We'll be through cleaning in a few hours. After that, it's yours. We were going to shampoo the carpets. Will that be a problem?"

"No, it will be late tonight or tomorrow before I can move anything in. It looks really nice. And with my grandparents five houses away, it'll work perfectly."

"Sounds like God's listening to both of our prayers today."

Tori smiled. "Yes, it does."

Chapter Seven

Steve arrived late Saturday afternoon, taking Tori by surprise. "I hardly have anything ready." She looked around the room filled with boxes. "I thought we agreed upon seven." She looked at her watch, confirming he was nearly three hours early.

"You want distance. It's probably best we skip dinner."

Surprise siphoned the blood from her face. She gave herself a moment to process what was happening. "Then why are you here? Why didn't you just call and say you couldn't make it?"

"I feel responsible for arranging this sudden move, and I'll follow through with my offer to help you get your things to Segundo. Even co-workers do that. We don't want to raise any eyebrows. Nothing unethical about it, right?"

She stepped back and brushed the hair from her face. "You wanted me to find a job and move back home. Why are you suddenly so angry that I'm doing it?"

"I'm not angry. Your points about the kids are valid. The supervisor issue—right again. Keeping our distance is better for everyone. I'm going to go home now." He walked through the maze of boxes. "Which ones can I take tonight?"

"Nothing. Don't worry about it."

"I didn't mean I'm not willing to help."

She took a step back. "It's fine, really. I'll get everything organized and have movers bring the furniture later in the week." She opened the door, hoping he'd leave before she made a further mess of their *non*relationship.

"I made an offer and I plan to stand by it."

"I'd say you've already done enough for my family. As it is, there's no way I can pay you. I tried and you tore my checks up in front of me."

"You paid me too much," he said sarcastically.

"You didn't give me a bill. I went on the going hourly wage, guessed on the supplies..." She hesitated, torn by conflicting emotions.

"I'll get around to writing one up. Until then, you don't owe me anything."

"And in the meantime you plan to keep showing up...unexpectedly with a helping hand?"

"'Like a bad penny,' you wanted to say?"

His sarcasm sent her head spinning. "You said it. I didn't."

"This is getting us nowhere. Order a pizza. That way I'll at least know you've eaten. We can load a few things while we wait for it to get here, and I'll be back tomorrow for the rest."

"I'll have movers bring the rest."

"It's not enough to bother with professional movers. Besides, it'll be much easier to maneuver a truck near the house without student cars in the lot." Tori had already packed her clothes, so the dressers were all ready to go. Together they carried them to the truck and found a few other small pieces that could fit in with the supplies he'd picked up for the ranch.

"So why are you the one always coming to the city for supplies for the ranch? Why doesn't Brody do that?"

"I enjoy the trip, and it works best for everyone. It's good to get out of the valley now and then, even though I don't want to live in the city."

She looked at him skeptically. "I suspect there's more to it than that, but whatever. Looks like dinner is here," she said, reaching into her pocket for the money.

Steve nudged her aside and reached for his wallet. "I'm paying this time."

"You paid last time. I found the money I gave you last time tucked under the place mat," she said, nudging him back.

"So I'm an old-fashioned guy. I'm not going to have a woman pay for my meal."

"It's a pizza! It's my house, and my move and I'm sick of arguing with you over everything. I'm paying. Besides, we're not dating." The kid got out of the truck, blissfully ignorant to the scene they'd just provided the neighborhood.

"Evening. Supreme on Chicago deep-dish crust?" he said, handing Steve the pizza. Tori handed him the money with a smile. "Thank you."

As they headed into the house, Tori laughed. "Was that so difficult to live with?"

"Guess it's the wave of the future, whether I like it or not. It would certainly raise a few eyebrows if I pay for a meal occasionally, wouldn't it?"

"When would you buy me a meal at work, anyway?"

"The staff likes to go out occasionally. Team building."

"It's good to hear they're friends as well as co-workers. So I guess Dutch treat is something you'll have to get used to." When they'd finished eating, Steve left.

Tori had called her grandparents twice already, and wanted to call again, but stopped herself from doing it. She'd have to learn to deal with the worry of them on their own if she was going to manage to work at all. They'll call if anything happens, she said to herself.

Tori found the smallest boxes and started packing books from her bookshelves. A piece of paper fell from her Bible, and she picked it up. It was a handwritten note, sent to her when she was in college. "'Do nothing out of selfish ambition, but in humility, consider others better than yourself.' Take God with you wherever you go, angel. Much love, *Abuela* Sandoval." Reassured that she'd made the right decision, the load seemed much lighter.

Determined to be ready when Steve arrived tomorrow, Tori worked late into the night packing. She made notes of people to call Monday to get the condo cleaned and ready for renters. While she waited for Steve to arrive Sunday afternoon, she went to the church service she'd attended years ago, wondering why she had stopped going. It wasn't like the one she'd been baptized into, but it was a strong Bible-teaching church and Tori liked it.

Steve's admonition hit the bull's-eye, reminding her of her shortcomings. She'd been too busy to get involved here. Much of her personal life had been ignored due to her late nights at sporting events, school activities or graduate classes. She wondered if she'd subconsciously chosen a large church where she wouldn't be missed. Over the years she had fallen away from regular church services. Sunday mornings she usually caught up on her housework and laundry. Maybe that, too, would change.

After saying goodbye to the few acquaintances who recognized her, Tori stopped at the hospital and visited Jerry Waterman, taking notes on his suggestions for reforming the school. He gave her insight on each staff member. "Normally, Tori, I'd let you figure them out for yourself, but these aren't normal circumstances." He took several deep breaths before trying to speak again. "If I remember correctly, the only absence you had in four years of high school was to stay home and take care of your grandfather after he caught pneumonia." He smiled sympathetically.

"And I thought you had some nerve giving me an unexcused absence for it," Tori said, remembering the scolding she'd received from the teachers. "*Abuela* had to work, and someone had to make sure he was okay."

"Truancy is one problem we haven't been able to change in all these years. Parents still don't understand that kids shouldn't be allowed to miss school to take care of younger siblings."

Tori shook her head. "We take care of our own. Family and God first."

"I'm sure you wondered how you'd be able to take care of your grandmother after her stroke, with your career so far away. God always provides, doesn't He? I'm so relieved you accepted the position. You'll do a great job."

"I'll give it my best, but remember, it's only temporary. We hope you'll feel like coming back soon."

"Don't hold your breath. It's going to be a while before I'm up to the task," he said. "You know where to find me if you need anything."

"Take care, Dr. Waterman."

"It's Jerry now, Tori. You're in charge."

When she got home Tori was more than surprised to find a rented moving truck sitting in front of her house. "Hi, Tori!" the kids both chimed.

They flew at her with welcoming hugs as if they hadn't seen her in months. "Hi, Kelsey, Kyle. What a nice surprise."

"Yeah, it was cool riding in a moving van!" Kyle exclaimed as if he'd just ridden a circus elephant. "Does this mean you're going to live with your grandparents all the time?"

"Close." She said, explaining that she would have her own house down the street so she could stay as close to them as possible. She looked up, even more surprised to see Brody climb out of the truck, followed by Steve.

"Should I presume this is your official acceptance?" Brody said with a smile. "Just to let you know, if there's anything personal going on between you two, well…if there is, I wasn't here. I knew nothing about it. And if anyone asks, you were my guest at my aunt and uncle's picnic, not this bum's." Brody threw a playful punch at Steve, and suddenly they looked more like teenage cousins than grown men.

Tori glanced at Steve. "Nothing to worry about, Brody. Your cousin isn't my type."

Brody laughed. "Right. Thanks for trying."

"Just because he seems to think he's my guardian angel doesn't make him one. And you can stop acting like one immediately."

"You don't want help moving?" Steve asked.

"I wasn't planning to move, until you had to mention the house that was available for rent. I'll hardly be there, anyway."

Steve unlatched the sliding door of the moving truck and pulled the ramp from the slot. "Why don't we finish what we came to do? The kids can carry some light boxes."

Tori punched in the code to her garage door, surprising them with neatly organized stacks of boxes ready to go. "Those in the front are priority, those along the wall can wait if necessary. We'll leave the refrigerator and appliances."

By dinnertime they were back in Segundo unloading her entire house. They helped her set up her bed and arrange the larger pieces, leaving the small stuff for her to do on her own.

Getting away had convinced herself that her grandparents were more capable than she'd wanted to think. They'd managed without help from her or anyone else, and even had dinner waiting when she returned Sunday night.

Drawing the lines in her and Steve's relationship was going to be difficult when her grandparents were constantly trying to play matchmakers. When she tried to explain that she and Steve couldn't get involved because of their working relationship, it was like talking to children. "You make such a cute couple," *Abuela* said, pinching her cheek.

Tori shook her head. It was useless.

First thing Monday morning Tori helped *Abuela* with her shower, then dropped her and *Abuelo* off at the therapy center in Trinidad for Maria's appointment. While there, Tori scheduled appointments for the next week.

The principal and superintendent of her previous school agreed to meet Tori at a restaurant halfway between towns to ease her tight schedule. In a matter of an hour they were able to settle the terms of her leave, sign papers and outline ideas for the school-to-school mentor program. By the time Tori returned to the therapy center, *Abuela* and *Abuelo* were worn-out. It took no effort to talk them into resting after they got home, which gave Tori a chance get ready for her meeting with the staff.

Tori stepped into the front doors of her alma mater Monday afternoon with an uncommon case of the jitters. She wasn't the valedictorian anymore; she was supposed to pull the staff and students together to save their school. Jerry's words echoed in her ears. *You're in charge now.*

More than once in the past three days she'd picked up the phone to refuse the offer. If it hadn't been for the unexpected move and rush of everything, she probably would have.

When the teachers filed into the cafeteria for their first meeting Tori felt the jitters fade. The staff looked as frightened as she'd felt. Brody had offered to be there to make introductions, but she'd declined. She was nervous, but there was no time for coddling insecurities.

Tori invited everyone to help themselves to the gourmet cookies and coffee that she'd picked up in the city for the occasion. After she'd made the rounds to speak to each teacher individually, Tori asked them to be seated. Within a few minutes everyone seemed at ease.

"Thank you for the warm welcome," Tori started. "As many of you know, I graduated from Coal Valley High School in 1988, and recognize a couple of faces from my time here. After graduation I attended the University of Northern Colorado, where I received my bachelor's degree in chemistry along with my teaching certificate. After two years of teaching, I completed my master's degree in educational leadership, also at UNC. Then I taught for five years in a Denver high school and I ventured into administration, and moved a little closer to home. I have been with Pikes Peak High School as an assistant principal for four years."

"Why in the world are you leaving one of the best high schools in the state to work here?" Tracy Hayes, a first-year teacher obviously hadn't heard the sequence of events that had brought her here, so Tori explained.

"While I'm very sorry to see Jerry Waterman ill and incapacitated, it's an honor to have the opportunity to return to my alma mater. Let me start out by saying that I do not have all of the answers, however, I will do all I can to help us find what works for Coal Valley Secondary School. We have a challenge ahead of us this year, and with the course that Jerry has laid out, I'm certain that we can make a huge difference in test scores. I want you to feel free to come to me at any time to discuss problems and ideas. My door's always open." She glanced around the table, her gaze lingering on Steve, and the jitters started again. She opened the large flip pad and wrote "Goals for Change" and the date. "I'd like to start out with each of you introducing yourself and giving me a quick glimpse of what you see as your role in the upcoming change at Coal Valley Secondary School. Fred, since you've seen the full range of successes at CVSS, would you start?"

"Fred Esquival. I've been at CVSS for twenty-six years, and I'd like to see us gain our students' respect again."

"Definitely a must. Any ideas of how we can do that?"

Fred looked around the room. "This is going to sound old-fashioned, but I think we need to let them know our expectations for them, and then hold them to it. Forget this policy of accepting late papers and re-taking of tests unless there are extenuating circum-stances."

"Thanks for your idea, Fred. I'm making note of your ideas and we'll discuss them at future planning meetings." She spoke as she wrote on the flip chart.

"Tracy…and just to help me out, would everyone re-mind me what subjects you're teaching this year."

"I'm Tracy Hayes. I'm a first-year English teacher. I believe that we're starting in the right place with inte-grating literacy across the curriculum. My husband, Gareth, is also a CVSS graduate, and we want CVSS to be here for our children, so I'm praying we can make a difference."

"Thank you, Tracy." Tori smiled at the innocence of a brand-new teacher. If only seasoned teachers could draw on that reserve of enthusiasm.

Before she could address the next teacher, Daria Chavez introduced herself and shared her goals for the year, and the introductions moved quickly around the table.

Soon they had a list long enough to turn another

page. "We're going to have a lot to discuss," Tori said as she tried to keep up. "Go ahead," she said as she kept writing, "I don't want to keep us too long tonight."

"Steve Remington, math teacher and administrative intern."

Tori was so surprised, she stared wordlessly at him, her heart pounding. She snapped her mouth shut before she said something to cause them both grief while the questions swirled around in her head. Why hadn't he told her before this that he wasn't just going to be a teacher here, but work closely with her?

"Would you like me to add my goals to the list for you?"

She looked around the room, feeling the blood rush back to her face. "That would be great." She handed him the marker. "Thank you."

She watched as Steve wrote "Clearer distinction between junior and senior high school" on one line and "Meet the needs of nontraditional students" on another.

"Those are monumental goals for one year," she said, disturbed that she'd missed his earlier comments. The other teachers seemed to approve, so she presumed the topics weren't new to the majority of the staff. "We'll see what we can do to address your concerns."

The last to speak was a retired reading specialist brought in to work with the teaching staff to help raise the Colorado Student Assessment Program—CSAP—scores. "I'm Geoff Gaffney. As most of you know, so I'll clarify for Tori, I've been hired as what is now called a 'literacy coach' to help teachers integrate read-ing and writing standards into everyday curriculum. I'll be here a couple of days a week to sit in on classes and work with each teacher, as well as to provide work-shops on teacher in-service days."

"Thank you, Professor Gaffney." Tori jotted notes on the pad and turned back to the group. "Before you panic, we aren't going to tackle any of these ideas today. I know that you've already had a long day.

"I'd just like to mention that literacy coaching helped Pikes Peak High raise scores by five percent, and I believe that CVSS students will show an even sharper increase. Over the next week, I'll be studying Coal Valley scores and visiting classrooms to get bet-ter acquainted." Tori glanced at her watch and set the marker on the table. "I make every effort to end meet-ings on time, so until our next staff meeting, feel free to drop in to my office."

While the teachers left, Tori cleaned the table and carried the flip chart to her office. She unlocked the door to the main office, not surprised to find Steve waiting inside.

"You could have warned me," she said quietly, seething with anger. "I knew it would be challenging to work together for the rest of the school year, but I didn't know it would be so closely."

"I had no choice," he said calmly, closing the hall door to the main office and opening the inner door to the principal's private office. She set her tablet inside her office door and stepped back into the main office.

He waited, but she wasn't about to invite trouble for her already vulnerable emotions.

"You had plenty of choices, Steve. Problem is, you selected the wrong one."

Chapter Eight

First thing the next day, Tori made the scheduled morning announcements, introducing herself to the student body. Steve saw the interest her voice over the loudspeaker raised from the teenage boys in his trigonometry class. Surely she knew there would be no work accomplished until everyone matched the undeniably feminine voice to their new principal. Proving her experience with teenagers, she called for a short assembly at the end of first hour.

He had fifty minutes to regain and hold the class's attention. "Okay, class, let's get to work."

"Come on, Rem, you don't expect us to do math now, do you?"

He could see right through the football star's game plan. Get the teacher talking about the new principal and steer him off subject long enough, and there'd be no use trying to accomplish anything for the rest of the hour. "No, Tommy. I expect you to spend the rest of the hour completing your trigonometry problems on page seventy-four. They're all review, so I don't suppose you should have any trouble completing them before the assembly. If you don't, you'll have homework."

A collective groan sent the classroom into an uproar. "Come on, Mr. Remington, what's the new principal like?"

"You'll see for yourself in an hour. If you don't settle down, I'll prepare a pop quiz for Thursday." As usual, his strategy worked. It only took once for the students to realize he didn't make idle threats. He wasn't about to get himself into describing Victoria Sandoval, or he wouldn't be able to concentrate for the rest of the day. As it was, he'd had trouble falling asleep last night, trying to erase the image of a very angry woman from his mind. He'd tried warm milk, classical music and even ran five miles on the treadmill after the kids had gone to bed. Nothing had helped.

Steve knew she had every right to be angry with him. He only hoped she'd come to understand how much he wanted her here. Badly enough that he'd kept his full title to himself for fear of frightening her away. Hopefully by the end of the year she wouldn't hate Coal Valley nearly as much as she thought she did. Hopefully she'd choose to stay.

Fifty minutes later he lined his students up at the door and led them to the gymnasium. She'd chosen a shapeless black suit with a white silk shell. She'd apparently learned long ago that one way to distract high school students was to dress like a bombshell. Her hair was tied back into a matronly bun at the nape of her neck, and she'd toned down her makeup to subtle attractiveness. He didn't think it possible to hide her beauty, but she'd accomplished the task. He smiled as he sat on the wooden bleachers, noting disappointment in the football star's reaction to her. The young man had produced a baseball cap, forbidden by the school dress code. "Hat please, Mr. Jiminez."

"C'mon, Rem. This isn't class."

"No hats in the school." He held out his hand for the student to hand it over, which he did. "Pick it up after school. If it shows up again, it's gone for the year."

"That's a new hat, man."

Steve wanted to laugh, but held it inside. "There's one way to keep it that way."

"I'd like to introduce myself," Tori yelled to the crowd.

The noise continued, and she waited patiently. After a few minutes of mild chaos, she placed her pinkie and forefinger into her mouth and whistled. An immediate hush spread through the gym.

"Thank you. Let's start over. I'm Victoria Sandoval, a 1988 graduate of Coal Valley Secondary School and I am honored to be back here as Dr. Waterman's temporary replacement." She moved with authority, the boxy look of her blazer helping to maintain the disguise of a stuffy old maid rather than the sassy woman with whom he thought he was falling in love. And right now he was very thankful for her modesty. The last thing the school needed was a massive crush on the new principal.

Despite her subdued appearance, the kids' applause seemed never ending. Being the first assembly of the year, he supposed the student body hoped this one to be more than simply to introduce the new leader. Tori reviewed her reasons for being here and gave the students an update on the principal's condition, which varied greatly from day to day. "I'm certain Dr. Waterman and his family would appreciate your thoughts and prayers. I'd like to encourage each of you to send him a card or letter. For those who are interested in doing so, I've spoken with Mrs. Hayes, and you will receive extra credit toward your English grade."

Again she received a round of cheers. Tori's personality was a perfect match for high school leadership. She connected well with the students. By the end of the assembly, she'd made an impression on every student in the room by inspiring them to reach for the stars, beyond their comfort zone, reminding them that they alone were the key to their future.

Steve finished his classes for the day, anxious to meet his new mentor, Principal Sandoval. He locked his classroom and headed to the main office to give Tori a bad time about how long she thought she could pull the wool over the sheep's eyes. He sauntered past the secretary to Tori's office. It was empty.

The secretary looked up from her desk. "Miss Sandoval is observing a class this hour. She left these data reports. She wants you to desegregate the data. Oh, and this goes with it."

He took the thick stack of paper and the accompany-ing CD-ROM, then looked at the young woman. "Do what with it?"

Carly Westbrook was nearly as new to the school as the layer of wax on the tile floors. She shrugged. "I hoped you knew what she meant. But that's what the note says."

"Oh," he said, looking at the note, "disaggregate."

"What in the world is that?"

"Separate in to components, like statistics for male students compared to female students, or special-needs students. I know what she means. I just can't quite be-lieve she wants me doing it," Steve said as he reversed his steps. "Did she say when…"

Carly turned to her notes. "Tomorrow at seven-thirty she'd like to review the notes with you, during your planning hour."

"Anything else?" he said sarcastically.

"You sure you want to ask?" Carly said with a sym-pathetic smile. "She has me digging through dusty boxes for old minutes and files. Count your blessings."

"Don't you just despise workaholic supervisors?"

"'Don't you just…'" Tori said from the hallway. "Get used to it, Mr. Remington. It's a job that never ends." She eased her way past him and into her office. "Carly, I'll be working on the attendance policy if you need me."

Steve considered following, but decided he'd save the razzing for another day. He'd already earned his first demerit for the day. Didn't need to add to his punishment. "I'll be working in the library, if anyone needs me."

Within the hour, Steve's eyes had crossed and he could hardly make out the fine print of the reports. "Do you happen to have a magnifying glass, Rose?"

"Shhh, Mr. Remington. There are students in the library."

"Sorry, Mrs. Ramirez." He corrected his informality, having forgotten school protocol to use proper names when school is in session or students are present.

"Let me look." She dug quietly through the drawers and shook her head. "They're gone. Would you like to use my magnifying glasses until you can get some of your own?"

He gave the older woman a playful glare, at which she laughed. "Sure. No need going blind on my first assignment."

Steve moved to a back corner of the room to avoid the noise, but didn't notice the school getting quieter until his cell phone rang. "Dad, are you coming to get us?"

He looked at his watch and jumped from his chair. "Kelsey, I'm sorry. I didn't notice it was so late. I'll be right there."

He stacked his papers and burst out the door, setting the alarm off. "Just what I need," he said, fumbling for his school keys.

"No problem, Mr. Remington. I'll turn it off for you," said the janitor.

"Thanks, Billy. See you tomorrow."

He'd never been so late to pick up his kids and couldn't figure out why they hadn't called earlier. He dialed the child care provider from his cell phone. "Bette, I'm terribly sorry. I'm on my way. How much do I owe you for overtime?"

"It's not a problem this time, Steve, but let's not make it a habit."

"You're a saint," he said, wondering how she could sound so cheerful at six-thirty, after dealing with a house full of kids throughout the course of the day. When he arrived at her house, he understood. He knocked on the door and stepped inside to two happy children and two friends.

"Sorry, Mr. Remington," Tori said to remind herself to keep their relationship on a business level. "I wondered just how long you'd sit in the library after the bells rang. I've got to go, Bette. Talk to you later." Again, she breezed past him, flaunting her perfection as Kelsey and Kyle hugged her, then Bette goodbye.

"Very funny." Steve didn't much appreciate his kids paying the price, though they looked like they'd had a fine time seeing Tori again. "Kids, you ready to go?"

"It wasn't a problem, Steve," Bette assured him. "Tori came over to catch up, and time got away from us, too. It wasn't intentional, just a perfect opportunity for her to get a little good-natured revenge for some comment you made today, I guess."

"So much for her sense of humor."

Bette laughed. "She knew you were joking with the

secretary, and if it hadn't been her first day on the job, she'd have laughed with you. I think she's more nervous about this monumental task than she wants to admit."

"We'll all sink or swim together. Since she's called a meeting at seven-thirty tomorrow, may I drop the kids off a few minutes earlier than usual. I don't want to be late after flunking my first assignment."

"Sure, see you guys tomorrow."

Steve had been up half the night writing an analysis of the data and still made it to the school on time. "Morning, Miss Sandoval."

"Good morning, Mr. Remington," she said with a smile. "You don't look nearly as tired as I suspected you might. Would you like a cup of coffee?"

"I'll save it for about one this afternoon. I'm still waiting on last night's caffeine buzz to wear off." He followed her into her office and set the summary on her desk. "Actually, I found the assignment very interesting—after I found a pair of magnifying glasses at the dime store."

"Can you believe the five-and-dime is still open, after all these years? Must be the only one in the country that is." She motioned toward the table across the room from her desk. "Why don't we work over there? It's a little more comfortable."

Tori took off the matching jacket to her dress and Steve noticed the outfit she wore today was more tailored than the one she'd worn to introduce herself to the school. Maybe she hadn't worn the baggy suit intentionally. He also noted she hadn't brought any personal items into the office as of yet. "How are your grandparents doing?"

She sat in the man-size executive chair and looked through the file drawer. "Fine, though I now know why I wasn't blessed with being a working mother. I thought I'd never get everything done this morning." She glanced up to him. "I don't know how you manage. You actually have to get your kids out the door with you in the morning."

He laughed. "We had a few late days in the beginning. Not to mention they were already used to the morning routine even before I was."

"Which reminds me, we'll need to go through schedules. I have a few days a week that I need to take *Abuela* to therapy, and she has a doctor's appointment to be scheduled soon. I'd like to minimize times when we're both out of the building." The more Tori talked, the more she seemed frazzled. "Where did I set those notes on the attendance policy?"

"You were working on them yesterday. Are they in your briefcase?"

She took a deep breath, closed her eyes and let out the breath. "No, I didn't think I'd have time to work on them, and I was right. Let's see, I worked on them up until Carly…" Tori jumped out of the chair and reached to the top of the filing cabinet. "Aha, I set them on top of the files. Sorry about the delay." She glanced at her watch. "Do we need to stop early for you to get ready for class?"

"That'd be nice, since I lost track of time and didn't get back to my classroom last night."

Her eyes shimmered with the light from the early-morning sun, and a giggle softened the seriousness of her expression. "I couldn't believe it when I saw your truck still over here at six. Then I walked down to my place, and it was still here at six-thirty, and…" She smiled openly at him. "It was easy to convince Bette to have a little fun with you. You did know she and I were good friends in high school, didn't you?"

"I think that did come up once, now that you mention it. Just remember, we have almost eight months left to work together. And you aren't the only one who likes practical jokes."

A faint blush shone along her cheekbones. "Just remember who signs your evaluation. Now what did you find on the reports?"

"What do you want to discuss first?"

She lowered her thick, black lashes. "What appears to have had the greatest effect on the testing?"

"Two factors," he said, appreciating her ability to return her focus to work. "Attendance and literacy."

Tori nodded. "In reviewing Jerry's notes, I see no mention of attendance being an issue."

Steve turned a few pages. "In the accountability data, we show two time periods of sharp decline in attendance."

"Fall and spring?"

Steve's jaw fell open. "How'd you know?"

"Could those time periods happen to coincide

roughly with harvest and calving seasons?" she suggested.

He looked at the spikes of absenteeism on the charts. "Could. So how'd you come to this conclusion?"

"When I was, oh, maybe a sixth grader, I recall school letting out for harvest days. And then when I worked at the ranch, I loved to ride along during calving. I wasn't one of the lucky ones to miss school for it, but I recall Brody missing several days. Then it became a holiday of sorts rather than a necessitated workday, and the district decided it was no longer necessary to build those days into the schedule."

"You're kidding. They gave kids days off to work?"

"Would I kid about data?" She went to her own minutes and found the sticky-note-marked absences. "How do you decipher this statement, 'Absences not in excess of the annual accepted percentage'? I read that to mean that for reporting purposes, they've averaged the spikes into the annual total, and diluted it to avoid having to pay the state back."

"If you knew this, why'd you have me stay up all night to evaluate it?"

"You're new, I'm new. We need tangible data to show the parents, teachers and the school board. This isn't going to be an easy problem to solve, even though the answer seems clear."

Steve shook his head. "Why hasn't anyone noticed this before?"

Tori leaned back in her chair. "Ever hear the adage, 'If it ain't broke, don't fix it'? It probably didn't matter to them, or the state for that matter, unless it was October first, when every student is counted for calculation of state funding. The rest of the year has been water under the bridge."

"When did the state begin recording attendance?"

"They only look at the average daily attendance, unless it's during CSAP testing. If we aren't testing ninety-five percent of our enrollment on testing days, that significantly impairs our scores."

"So what tricks are you going to pull to get kids in school during testing?"

She pulled out another report. "I don't believe in tricks." She leaned forward, explaining her proposal. "First, we have to sell the idea to teachers, get them behind us, then parents and, finally, if we have a train full of supporters, the school board can't turn us down."

"And I repeat, how do you plan to do this?"

"Give students one week off for spring break and another during calving season."

"Which is roughly during testing dates. How's that going to help?"

Tori thumbed through her folder. "That way, ranchers have the extra help they need, and in turn, the kids would have to come in outside traditional school hours to make up the time." She handed Steve a handout with three options for doing so.

"The board is never going to go for this."

"Even if I can prove nontraditional settings have huge success ratings across the state? Even if we can get parents behind us? Weren't you the one who suggested meeting the needs of nontraditional students? We've already lost two students to the mines this fall, according to our reports. With the economy hurting the way it is, that's not going to get any better."

Steve looked at her with renewed admiration. "If you can pull this off, it would be the answer to our prayers."

Before Tori could argue, the fire alarm sounded, and both of them jumped out of their chairs. "Where's the fire panel?"

"Don't know. Is it by the east doors?"

Tori and Steve headed toward the main entrance, and not finding a fire panel there, stopped back by the office. The secretary pulled her purse from her desk and headed out the door. "Miss Westbrook, would you please secure the office and make sure you have the master set of keys before you go outside?"

"Oh, yeah, do you want me to get your purse, too?"

"I didn't bring it today. Your station should be by the flagpole. Steve…"

"South exits."

"I'll be at the northwest exit." As Tori and Steve walked down the main hall, he looked to her. "Kitchen, lighter, or did someone just flat-out pull the alarm?"

"Pulled the alarm, but I don't know who yet. Any guesses on that one?"

"One. Corey Claiborne."

"No matter what you find out, publicly, this is a scheduled drill. If you see the janitor, find out where the panel is," she ordered as they came to the intersection where both had to check rooms and make sure their areas were clear. "Single file, kids."

Tori pulled one student from her locker. "No stopping. Get outside with your class."

"I have a graphing calculator in there. My mom'll…"

She paused long enough to pull the girl back into the stream of traffic and closed the locker. "If it's damaged in a fire, the school insurance will replace it. They can't replace you. Out."

Volunteer firemen pulled into the parking lot as Tori closed the last door behind her.

Chapter Nine

A week later Tori still didn't have enough evidence to prove who had pulled the fire alarm. The only drawback to the false alarm was filling out the required paperwork and wasting the volunteer firefighters' time and gasoline. Otherwise, it served as a reminder of how little responsibility Jerry Waterman had shared with his staff. Even though they couldn't justify paying a second full-time administrator, there needed to be a plan for emergency situations. "You don't see *anything* under crises management or emergency?"

"Nothing but an evacuation map," Carly answered, as if Tori was blaming her.

Tori shrugged. "I've looked through every document on the computer and every notebook in this office, and nothing. Maybe Jerry took it home with him to make revisions, but that does us no good. I need something to go on."

Steve walked through the main office into the teachers' workroom and returned with a cup of coffee. "What's up, ladies?"

Tori leaned against the counter. "Ever hear of a crises management manual?"

Steve took a sip of coffee and leaned against the doorjamb. "Of course I have."

Tori jumped to attention. "Do you know where we might find it?"

"Oh, you mean one for the school? No, never heard of it. I had one in my office in the army. Sorry. Need help looking?"

She shook her head. "We've searched everywhere. I really don't want to write one from scratch in two days. I have a meeting set up with Luis Martinez, the sheriff, for Wednesday afternoon, if you can make it. I need at least a rough draft to revise."

"Want me to dig into the computer?"

"I did a search for anything related to crises, management or emergency," Tori said, heading back to her desk. "Thanks, Miss Westbrook."

Carly, though young, proved to be a reliable and loyal helper. "I hope Mr. Remington has better luck than we did," she said. Like many in the small district, Carly wore two hats—health clerk and office manager. And considering she'd had one month of experience without a principal to actually run the office, Carly was a gem.

Tori backed through the doorway to say one more thing to Carly without realizing Steve was so close behind, and he ran right into her. "Whoa," he said, swinging his coffee cup away from both of them. "That was almost another disaster."

"Oops. Sorry. I needed to tell Carly something— both of you, really. I know I seem demanding right now, and I'm sorry. Once we get better acquainted with how the previous staff operated, I think it'll get easier for all of us."

She looked at Steve and waited for him to say something. "It doesn't bother me, Miss Sandoval."

"I slipped, didn't I?" Tori blushed, having forgotten school protocol. While there were no students here now, you never knew when one would walk through the door.

Tori returned to her office to find Steve had made himself comfortable in the executive's chair. She drank in the sight of his authoritative appearance, enjoying a quiet moment where no one could see her admiration. With her back to the public "eye," the moment was hers alone. Steve glanced up once and smiled as if nothing were out of the ordinary. "I'm not sure if you're aware that we are on a network."

She shook her head, disappointed that the moment of semiprivate time was gone. "Did you even hear my apology?"

"I hoped you realized Miss Westbrook and I were joking in the first place, but since you didn't, I accept the apology. Now, back to the network. Let me show you how to get there." He motioned for her to join him at the computer.

She leaned over his shoulder to get a better view of

the small screen, watching him delve into areas of the computer she didn't realize existed. With a few clicks, he'd found what she needed. "Voilà!"

"Oh my gosh! I can't believe it. You've saved me hours of work!" Her hand touched his shoulder as he opened the document and hit the print button.

Fred Esquival, the foreign language and American history teacher, rushed into her office unannounced. "Excuse me." Fred stopped at the door. "I didn't realize you two were busy."

Tori and Steve both looked up. She reached for the document on the printer.

Fred laughed, as if he felt the tension between Steve and herself. "I didn't mean to *interrupt* anything."

Tori stood, uncomfortable with the senior member of the staff acting as if he'd caught them behaving inappropriately. "Not at all," Tori said firmly. "What brings you here, Mr. Esquival?"

Steve stood to leave. "Call if that's not the report you need, Miss Sandoval."

Fred's bushy eyebrows resembled the hooded eyes of a hawk. "Don't leave on my account, Steve. I just came to welcome little Tori Sandoval to the staff. Is this a bad time?"

Steve paused midstep and Tori shook her head obligingly. "No, this is fine, but I'd appreciate it if you'd drop the adjective." She didn't like the lack of respect the term indicated.

Fred laughed. "Sorry, it's quite different having one of my students sitting in the principal's seat. It doesn't happen too often that a CVSS student goes away to college, let alone that one would come back to work on the staff."

"You know I like to beat the odds," Tori replied dryly.

Steve looked at her, then back to Fred. "So I imagine Tori was one of your finest students."

Fred's smile showed his irritation. "Yes, she was, but a little big for her britches, even then. Her grandparents came to parent-teacher conferences with young Tori once. I explained my grading policy, and Tori looked right at me and told me she was *not* doing extra credit work just to get an A in my class."

"I aced every assignment. I deserved an A without needing to complete extra credit work. And it was the only B on my transcript," Tori said, forcing a smile and laughing. She still didn't agree with contract grading for the general populous.

Steve joined the laughter, though he clearly didn't understand what they were referring to.

"Well, I just wanted to stop in and say hello," Fred said, moving to leave. "You two carry on with whatever you were doing." He walked out, closing the door behind him.

Tori took a deep breath and let it out. She dropped in to the chair, leaned her elbows on the desk and rested her forehead in her hands. "Tell me I'm not imagining what just happened. Did Fred try to undermine my position?"

Steve reached for the string to close the shade on her door.

"Don't," she said quietly. "Fred is going to try to fuel any fire he can against me, and I don't need rumors to spread that we're involved. It's probably best if you leave me alone now."

Steve nodded and reached for the doorknob. "For your information, I don't want to leave right now. Off the record, I want to come over there and hold you and tell you what a wonderful job you're doing. May I call you tonight?"

She nodded. "I get Grandma and Grandpa into bed about ten and walk to my place."

"Why don't you call me when it's convenient, then? You need my home number?"

"It's in your file."

When Tori walked out her grandparents' door to leave that night, she knew she didn't have the time or energy to rehash what had happened that afternoon. She called Steve and quickly thanked him for the moral support, then begged out of visiting in order to work on the crises manual for the next teacher meeting. She could tell he wasn't happy with her excuse, but he respected her enough to agree with her decision.

Tori dropped onto the sofa and looked around. She'd managed to get the furniture into their proper rooms, but as for aesthetics, the house needed work. For over a week now, she had come home just in time to drop into bed. Tomorrow morning she needed to take Grandmother to therapy, which meant she didn't have to be at the school until after lunch. She carried the boxes to the room where they belonged and moved the furniture. No matter how she arranged it, something wasn't right.

The phone rang and her heart stopped. Who would call this late? "Hello," she said with urgency.

"Tori, are you okay?" Her mother's voice always surprised her. Tonight, it was almost a relief to hear from her parents. It had been nearly two weeks since they'd called.

She knew it would be a long conversation and settled into the sofa once more, covering herself with a down comforter. "I'm fine, Mom. You just startled me. I thought something was wrong with *Abuela*."

"No, she's fine. I just called there, and they gave me your new phone number. What happened? I thought you were staying in your old room."

Tori caught her parents up on her grandparents, the house and the challenges of her new job. By the time she'd finished, she couldn't sit still. While they talked, Tori began unpacking boxes of kitchen items.

"I can't believe Mr. Esquival is still teaching," Tori's mother said, "let alone that he remembered you refusing to do extra credit work." Her mother laughed. "I must admit, though I couldn't believe you did it, I was shamefully proud of you for standing up for your beliefs, even if it cost you."

"Throwing it in my face is more like it. It won't be two hours before everyone in the school has heard about it."

Her father chuckled over the extension. "Oh, my

niña, God knows what He's doing in your life, don't you worry."

"Trial by fire it feels like."

"God blessed you with many gifts, Victoria, but he expects much in return from you, as well. You know He won't give you more than you can handle."

"*Abuela* said something about you and the Remington boy seeing each other again, her father said."

Tori dropped the plate she'd unwrapped and shards of glass flew everywhere. "No, I'm not dating anyone. She's talking about Steve Remington, Brody's cousin from back East somewhere. He's a teacher at the high school, and an administrative intern for the school, but we're not dating." Tori looked in each room for a broom and dust pan, finally locating them down the hall.

"Though you'd like to?"

Why her parents were so caught up on her life suddenly, she wasn't sure, but she didn't feel like arguing with them tonight. "He's the one that built the ramp for *Abuela,*" she said, hedging their question. "And he happened to be driving through town when he saw *Abuelo* at the store and gave him a ride home. It's just been odd circumstances that have made it look like he's interested, but…"

"Oh, Tori. You don't want someone—"

"Don't even say it, Mama. I'm not chasing anyone. Besides I have a career, and my own house and I can date a man from the other side of the tracks if I want to now." Well, I could if he didn't happen to be working for me, she reasoned.

"But, Tori, you know better than to fall into—"

"It's not even an issue. I'm in the middle of a sea of glass here, Mama. I need to clean it up and get to bed. And don't worry about me falling in love with the wrong person. I'm thirty-four and I haven't rushed into anything yet, have I?" She hated that she had so little patience with her parents on certain issues. Tori knew when to end the conversation before anyone could say something they would later regret.

Tori suspected it came from their repeated attempts to parent her from two thousand miles away. Every year, they'd joined members of their church to go on missions. Every year, their love of the job kept them away longer and longer.

She finished emptying the box of dishes, swept and mopped the floor, vacuumed the nearby carpet and still couldn't take her mind off her parents' phone call. No matter how much she accomplished, she always seemed to fall short in their eyes. She became a teacher, and they'd said, "We're proud of you, Victoria, but you could do so much more good teaching orphaned children in other countries." She taught in the inner city, and again, she should've reached out to those even less privileged. She remembered the first year they had joined a long-term mission, and they'd taken Tori and her brother with them. Two months later, Tori begged them to send her home, and they had. Her grandparents' tiny house had seemed like heaven after the hut her family had shared with another missionary family.

Tori admired her parents for having the heart to give

so much of themselves to the needy. She eventually came to the conclusion that Victoria Sandoval simply hadn't been so gifted. She had believed for a while that giving back through teaching would show her parents that she, too, had a "mission field," but somehow it never measured up in their eyes.

Yet tonight, they almost led her to believe that they approved of her choices. That is, until they'd heard about Steve. Whether it was the fact that he wasn't Hispanic, or that his family had money, or simply that his extended family had once been her family's employer, she wasn't sure. Maybe it was all of that.

Tori looked at the clock and forced herself to go to bed. She couldn't sleep, and recalled a line from a song in a favorite movie. It talked about counting blessings instead of counting sheep when you're worried and can't sleep. She closed her eyes and finally dozed off somewhere in the middle of her talk with God, thanking Him for each blessing in her life.

The attendance project had been forced to take a back seat while the first item on the agenda for the staff meeting focused on safety issues and emergency preparedness.

"We never had to waste our time with those details before. Jerry handled all of that. Why change it now?" Fred complained.

Tori knew it was only a matter of time until Fred found something to complain about. She patiently explained her reasoning. "With such a small staff, we don't have the luxury of sharing this load among administrators. I believe an issue as important as safety procedures should be a priority for all of us." She saw several heads nod and turn to the troublemaker of the staff.

Fred crossed his arms across his chest and frowned. "You didn't answer my question."

"There are going to be changes, and I'm sure we'll all adjust to them with a little effort," Tori responded.

Fred didn't miss a beat. "Jerry wouldn't have—"

"This isn't up for discussion, Fred. If you have a problem with the job of protecting our students, we can discuss it with the school board since our superintendent is still in the hospital. In the meantime, I've been hired to do a job, and that means there will be a few changes."

Steve smiled and several teachers stifled their laughter.

Fred pouted and for a moment, she wondered if he was going to get up and walk out of the meeting. Since it appeared Fred had quieted for the moment, she continued speaking.

"Steve and I have updated the emergency plan with the help of Luis Martinez, Segundo sheriff. You have a copy in the red binder and it's your responsibility to read and follow the guidelines by the end of the week. If there are any questions, either Steve or I will be happy go over them with you."

She reported on the time it took them to clear the building after the fire alarm. "Not bad for our first evacuation, but for a building this size, I think we should be able to cut our time in half. I've scheduled another drill for Monday. Our goal is two minutes."

Fred cleared his throat. "We have drills every year. What's the big deal?"

Tori ignored his rhetorical question. "As you're aware, we're required by law to have four drills per year. Please go over the rules with students and remind them that we do not go to our lockers for anything after the alarm rings."

Jason Hunt, the physical education teacher, raised his hand. "Who are the suspects, and what is the punishment going to be?"

"We don't have substantial evidence to penalize anyone, so I don't think it's fair to announce any names. If anyone hears anything you think is pertinent, let me or Steve know."

She barely had time to explain the charts on the attendance policy before it was time for the meeting to adjourn. She considered waiting another week to open it for discussion, but needed to get moving on it. She looked at her watch and passed the report around the table. "I want to explain this report very quickly. Please read it carefully before our next meeting. We'll discuss it more thoroughly then. It is not an approved change yet. In order for it to ever change, we need to approach the parents and the school board with a viable plan. Steve, will you please explain the reports."

Tori took a seat and Steve presented the information with mathematical logic. No one argued with a word he said.

Things went smoothly for the next few days, and less than two weeks later, they had the support from almost a third of the parents for the new attendance policy. Tori was thrilled with the turnout at the parent meeting, and though she had hoped more would sign the letter of interest, she felt certain that support would spread. If the board approved the plan, they would offer a few evening classes beginning next semester.

Two days later, the discussion returned to the fire alarm investigation. She had yet to get a confession out of their only suspect, Corey Claiborne. A loner, Corey seemed an unlikely culprit. He wasn't even scheduled for class at the time the alarm sounded, yet there were several reports that he'd been seen on campus a few minutes before school started.

She looked at the names of the other two students who had hall passes during first hour. One was an office assistant, and the other an athlete who had everything to lose if found guilty. Though pressure mounted to find the offender, Tori wouldn't give in unless they had a confession. "We've discussed this a million times, Steve. What makes you so sure Corey did it?"

Steve looked at the pictures of Corey in the yearbook and read through his squeaky-clean file. "I'm not really sure. Too quiet, maybe. He's grown up here, and he doesn't belong to any of the organizations, doesn't show any interest in sports and has no friends. Why?"

Tori didn't want to offer a guess. She could empathize with the Coreys of the world. She'd had friends, but she was also more of a loner than anything. "Maybe he has interests that don't lend themselves to groups. Like art, or drawing, or reading…" she suggested.

Steve looked up to her. "Could be. It could also be a way to get attention. Or, hopefully not, a way to get back at those who don't see things the same way he does." Tori closed Corey's file.

"It was a fire alarm, not bombs or guns. Kids have been pulling this prank for decades."

"Shouldn't we consider why he or she pulled the alarm?"

"I think you're overreacting."

Steve shrugged. "I hope so."

"Besides, Corey has never been in any trouble. He has no referrals. I'd like to wait. Maybe the culprit will think they've gotten away with it and start bragging." Tori leaned against the table that had become a comfortable barrier between them. It seemed the minute they sat across from one another here, their focus was on business, not on what couldn't be between them.

"Aha, the tried-and-true 'loose lips sink ships' tactic."

She smiled, liking his look of approval. "There is a reason it's tried and true. Kids can't keep their exploits quiet forever. Not even loners."

Chapter Ten

A week later Carly tapped on Tori's office door. "Sorry to bother you, Miss Sandoval. We have a situation that needs your attention. Marcus was involved in a fight, and Mr. Esquival sent both students to see you, but only Marcus came in. I've bandaged his wound."

Steve saw a glint of worry in the secretary's panicked expression. "You okay, Miss Westbrook?"

She nodded.

"Would you like me to take care of it?" Steve offered, hoping to put out the fire Fred was trying to light under Tori's career. "Mr. Esquival didn't bring both students down?"

"I haven't seen Mr. Esquival, only Marcus."

Tori began clearing the table and looked at the young man through the window on the door. "I think we'd better handle this together. Did you see the other student?" She moved her notes to her desk.

"I saw someone run out the main doors to his car and speed off. I assume it was the other student involved, but I'm not sure," Carly said with a shrug.

"Does Marcus need further medical attention, Miss Westbrook?"

"I believe so. The bleeding is under control as long as he keeps pressure on it, but the one gash is pretty deep. I sent the office assistant to the coach's office for an ice bag."

"Call his parents. See if one of them can get here to take him to the clinic. If not, we'll have to call an ambulance," Tori instructed. She moved from the table to her desk. "Go ahead, Steve. I'll take notes."

"Should I send him in now?"

"Yes, please," Steve said, moving one of the chairs across from Tori's desk.

As the boy made his way past Carly Westbrook, she reminded Marcus to keep applying pressure to his cut. "I'll get you some clean gauze. Which parent should I call?"

"Oh, man, you don't have to call them, do you?" He slammed a fist against the door.

Steve stepped closer to the young man. "Drop the temper, Marcus. It's only going to make matters worse. According to the law, we have to inform parents if their child is injured or involved in a fight. You may need stitches. Miss Westbrook, call both parents. Let them decide who can come."

"They'll ground me for a month, and it's gonna be your fault," he said, looking at Tori.

"Your choices brought you in here today, Marcus, not me. Why don't we sit down and talk? Miss Westbrook, would you see if Mr. Esquival can join us please? I believe Ms. Chavez has planning this hour. See if she can cover his class."

After Steve had asked a couple of questions, he determined that Marcus probably wouldn't have been cut if Mr. Esquival had followed proper procedures.

"Were there others involved in this argument besides you and Miguel?" Tori interrupted.

"No, it's a family matter between him and me."

Mr. Esquival entered the office and Tori took a deep breath. Steve wanted to handle this matter, and it looked like it was killing her to remain silent.

Steve jumped right in before Tori had a chance. "Mr. Esquival, were you aware that Miguel had a knife?"

Fred looked horrified. "No. It was just a fistfight."

"Was there any specific reason you didn't escort them both to the office?" Steve said calmly, giving Fred plenty of clues that he'd better have a very good reason for not doing so.

"Class was just starting, and I was concerned that the whole class would get riled up."

"I see. Did they?"

"No, because I was there to take control."

"So there are no further issues we need to deal with immediately?"

Fred shook his head.

"Can you confirm for us who the other student involved was? He never made it to the office."

Fred named the same student that Marcus had. "Please go back to class, Mr. Esquival, and we'll speak with you again during your planning hour. We need to finish talking to Marcus before his mother arrives to take him for medical attention."

Without a word, Fred left. Tori jotted notes on her electronic organizer while Steve asked more questions. "Marcus, what started the argument?"

The kid looked at the floor, ignoring their question. "None of your business."

"You made it our business the minute you two started fighting on school grounds. Who started the fight?" Again, silence. After several more attempts to get answers, Steve informed him that he would be suspended from school, and they would let him know the duration after they talked with Miguel.

"I started it," he said, puffing his scrawny chest out. "I warned him to stay away from my sister."

"Did he hurt your sister?"

"Not yet, but he's a two-timing waste of—"

"I get the idea, Marcus," Steve said before the kid had the chance to finish the insult. From there on Marcus answered his questions without hesitation. The discussion with Marcus's mother went well, and they scheduled another appointment for later in the week to set up disciplinary action.

After they left, Steve looked to Tori and shrugged. "How'd I do?"

"Great," she said, offering a couple of suggestions. "Unfortunately, this problem is far from settled. We have Miguel to find, Fred to reprimand and a young girl to counsel before Marcus's fears become reality." Tori jotted more notes, then lifted her head. Worry lines replaced the smooth skin of her forehead and he wished he could erase them for her.

"I'll call Miguel's parents, ask if they've seen him since the incident. Since that probably won't get us very far, I think we should call in the sheriff. Let them find him. With this snowstorm rolling in, I don't want any of us out on the roads. Aunt Elaine says we already have six inches at the ranch. And since Miguel had a knife, it's an automatic expulsion, anyway."

She lifted an eyebrow. "Authoritative, decisive and up on the law. Very impressive."

He stood, trying to keep his mind off how he'd like to thank her for the compliment. He tipped his head, and she smiled. "I'll call the police," Steve said. "Do you want to be there when I talk to Fred?"

The smile disappeared. "Not especially, but this is a serious enough issue that I need to handle the discussion. It has nothing to do with your capabilities, understand. I can't avoid a letter in his file for this one. Three strikes."

"You mean you're going to fire him?"

She shook her head and looked out the window. "That depends on Fred. If this insubordination continues, that's a definite possibility."

Steve had been ready to leave, but closed the door again and picked up the phone. "Let me call the sheriff real quick, then let's talk." He looked at his watch as he waited for the dispatcher to transfer his call to Luis. "Why don't we eat in here? Fred's planning hour is right after lunch." Sheriff Martinez came on the line and Steve explained the incident.

While he discussed the situation with Luis, Tori went to Carly's desk and called her grandparents to see how they were doing, not surprised that things were running smoothly there. She apologized that she wouldn't be able to come by after the lunch hour. Then she called the café and ordered four daily specials, requesting that they be delivered to the main office at the school.

"Miss Westbrook, Mr. Remington and I are going to be discussing this morning's incident over lunch, and barring another emergency, we…"

Carly pressed her lips together, trying not to smile. "I'll take messages for you."

"It's a business meeting."

"Surely I'm not the only one who thinks you would make a cute couple."

Tori looked in the teacher lounge and out in the hall. "I would not know about that. There is nothing personal between us," she said, noting the disappointment on Carly's face. "And won't be while we're working in the same school. Professionally, it would be suicide."

Carly shrugged, a smile sneaking back into her expression. "Doesn't seem to matter to the staff. I hear that Daria's even backed off of Steve. Apparently she's been chasing him since he started teaching here last year."

Tori tried to contain her surprise. "I'm not accustomed to choosing dates by popular vote, but thanks, anyway."

"You don't have a date for Homecoming, do you?"

"I hadn't planned on one, either. How did we end up with Homecoming in November, anyway?"

"They postponed it, hoping Dr. Waterman would be better." She pulled out her notebook. "You do know that the staff helps the parents' committee serve the dinner, don't you?"

"No, that's new, isn't it? In my time couples went into a restaurant in town before the party."

She nodded. "Yeah, but parents felt this would cut down on accidents and well, *accidents*. Fund-raising covers a steak dinner in the cafeteria. I'm in charge of staff assignments. You'll help, won't you?"

"Sure. How'd you get the job if it's organized by the parents?"

Carly smiled. "I'm the staff liaison."

"Luis will call us when he's contacted Miguel," Steve said as he walked out of her office. "Want me to go get us a couple of plates before the bell rings?"

The delivery person from the café drove up to the school. "No thanks. Lunch is here." Tori rushed outside before the delivery girl got out of her car. Steve followed, holding the door open for her. Tori took two containers and asked that she deliver the other two dinners to the white house across the street, handing her an additional tip.

"I thought we agreed it's Dutch from here on," Steve

said once Tori stepped back inside and stomped the snow from her dress boots. She'd obviously heard the weather report, as she was wearing a long black wool skirt and a Native American-motif wool blazer over a cashmere turtleneck.

"It is, and you owe me four dollars." She walked into the office, turning her head in his direction. "Could you get me a can of tea from the refrigerator in the teacher's lounge?" While he was gone, Tori had made room for their meals, moving the piles of files and papers to the floor behind her desk.

Steve looked at the desk, then at the round table just a few feet away. "Why don't we sit over there?"

"Because that looks 'cozy' and this looks 'business' and maybe, just maybe, it will help us keep it that way."

Steve took a seat across the desk from her, disappointed that she'd drawn a definite line between them. "We don't have much time, so what are you thinking in regard to Fred's actions?"

"I'm thinking I should have written this letter after the teacher meeting. And I wish I could find out if Jerry had problems with him. If he did, there's no evidence of it in his file, but Brody alluded to the fact during our initial meeting for the job. There has to be record of it somewhere."

"You think Jerry's too soft?"

She looked up from her green-chile-topped tamales and nodded. "But that's not the issue now. If we let this slide, Fred's not going to ever take me seriously. And the other teachers won't, either." She set her fork down and spun the chair around, looking across the parking lot to her grandparents' house. "I finally felt as if I'd gained the teachers' trust. If I fire Fred, they'll think I'm a ruthless dictator. Do you think it's too soft to put him on principal-directed goals?"

Steve hesitated, then took another bite to think a little longer. "I think so. You can't forget that his dereliction of duty could cost the district if Marcus's parents sue. You have to take a firm approach, Tori. Everyone is watching to see how you handle him. After the incident at the teacher meeting, he's lost a lot of respect from his peers. And I'm not sure if you're aware that yesterday morning, he told your story in the teacher lounge."

She closed her eyes. "I can't believe he's doing this."

"You sure you didn't slit the tires on his car or something more than tell him you didn't want his lousy A?" Steve smiled.

"Nothing. It's almost like he's trying to get me fired. And right now I'm so on edge, I don't even care if it's him or me."

Tori heard Carly telling someone that Tori was in a meeting. Seconds later Fred Esquival barged into the office. "I should've figured. Cozy lunch, trying to plot how to get rid of the old man again. Let's get this over with so I can see my lawyer."

Tori stood. Noticing the wide-eyed teachers peeking around the corner from the teachers' lounge, she walked over and closed the door. "If that's your attitude, Fred, maybe it's best we reschedule this meeting until you've had time to calm down and bring a representative with you. Save us all some time." She sat on the corner of her desk.

"One mistake and you're canning me?" He ranted on as if he really thought tenure could protect him from losing his job over a lawsuit.

Tori waited several minutes to see if he was ready to listen, then lowered her voice. "No one wants to fire you, Fred," she said with a quiet emphasis on the word *want,* though he probably didn't notice anything with the steam he was blowing out his ears.

"Today's incident isn't the first since I've arrived on the job, but it was a serious mistake that legally I can't overlook. Escorting students involved in any kind of conflict to the office is not a new policy. It's been common practice since I attended here. So maybe you'd like to explain again why you didn't follow policy?"

"I felt it was more important to keep my class under control," Fred yelled, his voice cracking. "I told you, there's no respect in this building. Kids think they run the place."

"What are you talking about?"

"Some juvenile delinquent sets off the fire alarm and you did nothing, just like you used to mouth off sixteen years ago, and no one did anything to put you in your place."

Tori froze and Steve stepped between them. "You're way out of line, Fred."

Fred picked up the small statue of the school mascot from the shelf behind him, stepped aside and pitched it at Tori. She ducked, and it knocked the shade from the hinges and broke the glass insert on the oak door between Tori's office and the main office.

Tori stepped behind the desk. "This meeting is over, Mr. Esquival. I think you'd best take a few days of personal leave to think about your future as a teacher."

"I'm not taking any personal leave. You want me out of here, fire me!"

Tori sent him a calculated warning. "I will be contacting the school board, and I think it would be wise for you to contact your teachers' association representative."

She watched Steve escort Fred out of the building, then took a deep breath. Tori opened her file drawer and pulled out the substitute teacher list. She had no sooner picked up the phone to start making phone calls than several teachers filed into her office.

"Are you okay?" Angelia Casale offered Tori an unopened can of pop. "Need something to drink?"

Tori smiled, but shook her head. "Thanks."

"I have last hour free. I'll cover his class," Jason Hunt offered. "And if you have trouble replacing him, I'll volunteer to give up my planning hour to teach his American history classes. That was my minor, so I'm already certified."

She thought Jason had been a cohort of Fred's. "Thanks, Mr. Hunt, but he hasn't been fired yet."

"What do we need to do to make it final?" Daria asked, crossing her arms across her plush bosom. "I've taught next to him for twelve years, and I can vouch for the fact that it's long past time someone get him out of here. He's cancer to this school's future."

"You have our full support," Jason added.

"Thank you," Tori said, fighting tears. The bell rang.

Angelia gave Tori a hug. "Let us know what we can do, seriously." The teachers turned and headed back to class.

Tori looked at the calendar. It was Thursday, and Monday was an all-day teachers' workshop. If the staff could cover Fred's classes today, find a substitute for to-morrow, hopefully the board would have a decision in time to locate a permanent sub for the remainder of the year.

"Miss Sandoval?" Carly peeked around the corner. "Steve, um, Mr. Remington said he'd be back after his class. Would you like me to call the custodian to re-place the window?"

Tori smiled. "Yes, thank you, Miss Westbrook." She started picking up the larger pieces of glass when the phone rang.

"It's Brody Remington for you, Miss Sandoval."

Tori stood and dropped the pieces into the trash can. "News travels fast. I'll take it in my office. Would you see if the janitor is available to finish picking up the glass?"

"Hello, this is Tori."

"I warned Steve that you were a heartbreaker. Guess I should have made it a public announcement, huh?" Brody had the nerve to laugh. "Guess we'd better get our ducks in a row, hadn't we?"

Tori turned her back to the mess, hoping the snow-flakes drifting to the ground would soothe her nerves.

"I'm sorry, Brody. I didn't see this coming. I thought he was just pushing to see how far I'd bend. I didn't know he had it in for me. For the record, which version have you heard, Steve's or Fred's?"

"Neither. Your secretary called me in a panic as the mountain lion hit the window. Anyone hurt?"

"Physically, no." She rubbed her forehead with her hand. "While you're sitting down, did you hear about the knifing that led up to it?"

"The what?" There was no humor in his voice now.

"Why don't I finish typing up my notes on the report and I'll e-mail them to you. We have Sheriff Martinez looking for the student who injured the other kid."

"The sheriff was called? Why wasn't I informed earlier?"

"We've been a little busy with damage control."

"Sorry," he said. "Joking aside, is there anything I can do?"

"Tell me where I can find Fred Esquival's real file. I have four staff members up in arms to have him fired on the spot, but there's nothing in his record for at least the past five years. Somehow I don't believe he could have held his temper for that long."

"I'll be right there."

"No, Brody. There's no need coming here now. My office is a shambles, there's no privacy to talk and the teachers are upset. Even Jason Hunt has cut all ties with

Fred. He's volunteered to cover his classes for the remainder of the year. I'm calling a staff meeting after school. What do I tell them?"

"You tell them that the school board will stand behind you. We'll take immediate action. In the meantime, don't let anyone touch a thing in the office. I think we'd better file another report with Luis."

Chapter Eleven

Tori didn't argue when Steve asked if he and the kids could bring steaks over for dinner with her and her grandparents. She needed a buffer, and kids served as excellent deterrents from going through the grisly details of the day. While Steve was there, Luis Martinez stopped by with information on Miguel's arrest, Bette called to check on Tori and several parents who had heard bits and pieces of information from their children on the events of the day called to voice their opinions. By the time she and Steve had handled all of the calls, it was ten o'clock and his kids had fallen asleep watching television with her grandparents.

Abuelo looked at Tori. "I don't think you should be in your place alone tonight, angel. Why don't you stay here?"

"I was going to suggest Steve tuck the kids into the twin beds in the guest room and he sleep in my old room." She looked into his eyes, thankful for his friendship. "By the time you get home and come back in the morning, you'll barely get five hours of sleep. And this snow isn't letting up."

"I'm with your grandfather. I don't want you down the block alone tonight. The snow isn't expected to stop until tomorrow night. Why don't you stay here and I'll sleep at your place?"

She laughed. "No. If anyone's going to do damage, I'd just as soon the house be empty. I don't want anyone hurt. You take my bed here, and I'll sleep on the sofa. It's very comfortable."

"You drive a hard bargain. Sold."

Steve helped Tori make the beds then tucked Kelsey and Kyle in for the night. While she helped her grandparents get settled, Steve watched the news. "Thank you for inviting us to stay in town tonight."

She glanced at the space next to him on the sofa and decided not to tempt herself. She sat in the recliner across the tiny room. "I feel better all the way around. I'm glad that you're not driving home in the snow, and I feel safer with you here."

"I'm not so sure about that. I didn't do much to deflect the mountain lion from flying at you."

Tori shook her head, still in shock over the day's events. She felt a chill bolt up her spine. "It's like he was on drugs or something. He may not have been the easiest person to work with, but he wasn't a bad teacher."

"Did Brody mention talking to Jerry about it?"

"We have a football game in Widefield Saturday

morning. I scheduled an appointment to show my condo after the game. Then I thought I'd go talk to Jerry in person."

"Would you like company? Unfortunate as it is, this is a great training opportunity."

She and Steve talked late into the night. They turned out the lights and from the matching set of recliners facing the window, they watched the snow fall against the lights of the school.

"Wouldn't it be a blessing if the superintendent canceled school tomorrow?" Tori said with a giggle. "We could play board games all day, just like when I was a kid."

"You seem to have forgotten one problem."

Tori closed her eyes. "What's that, Mr. Know-it-all?"

"We don't have a superintendent at the present time."

She pulled her legs to her body and tugged the quilt around her shoulders as the wind whistled through the windows. "Then you can call your cousin and insist he call a snow day."

"From your grandparents' house? Wouldn't he love that one?"

"He's not the only one," Tori said with a smile.

Steve stood and stretched. "I'm going to hit the sack. See you in the morning."

"I guess God heard your prayers," Steve whispered early Friday morning. He knelt next to the sofa. "Brody canceled school. We need to call teachers."

Tori sat up and looked outside. "Wouldn't it be nice if it could stay this quiet and peaceful all day?" She looked at the set of tire tracks in the parking lot. "Who's been to the school already?"

"Probably the custodians. Doesn't Billy get there about five?"

"No, he usually comes strolling in about six. What time is it?" She reached for her watch, brushing against Steve's arm on the way. "Excuse me."

He stood and backed away. "It's only five-thirty. You call the staff and I'll go check the school. It'll look better to have the truck there instead of here, anyway."

"I'll be over in a while, then. Thanks." Tori found her PalmPilot, opened the file of staff phone numbers, called the teachers and gave them the good news. Then she took a quick shower and dressed.

"Tori, is everything okay?" *Abuelo* called from their bedroom.

"Brody called a snow day, but Steve went to check the school. I'm going over now and we'll be back in a bit."

Quickly realizing her snow boots were down the block at her house, Tori tugged on her tennis shoes and coat. She trudged down the driveway and into the drifts of snow blown across the street. She saw Steve's truck by the school's front door, but flashing lights caught her attention. She turned to see where they were, not terribly surprised to find them in front of her rented house. She ran.

Steve rushed out of her house and met her at the

gate. "Tori, don't come in." The wind blew the hood off her head and Steve pulled it back on, tying the strings under her chin.

"Never mind the hood. What happened?" She leaned to the side to look around him. "Steve, let me go. I need to see what happened."

"Luis is here and needs to get pictures first."

Her imagination moved from slight vandalism to real fear. "How bad is it?"

"Let's just say I'm glad no one was here last night."

She realized how close she'd come to ignoring her fears and going home. "Any damage at the school?"

"Someone threw a rock through your office window."

She shook her head and pushed her way past Steve. "Any idea who would have done this?" she asked as the sight of her shredded sofa hit her like a blow in the gut. Her mouth fell open.

"Well, we have a few people on our list after yesterday," Luis said as he came around the corner from the bedroom. "Footprints at the back door give an idea of his shoe size, but unfortunately, it's a pretty common size, and the snow may have filled them in a bit."

"Any fingerprints?"

Luis shrugged. "We don't have the expertise to handle anything like this. I'm calling the Colorado Bureau of Investigation to send an investigator. This wasn't a random act. You were obviously the target."

Tori shuddered. "Did you find Miguel?"

"Arrested him yesterday evening," Luis said. "He's

out of the picture. His mother couldn't post bail. So our prime suspects are Fred and Marcus. Have you had any other incidences at the school lately?"

Steve waited, but Tori couldn't speak. "A fire alarm a couple of weeks ago, and the sprinklers came on during the first football game, but the custodian was sure he'd turned them off the night before. No one was hurt, and we couldn't prove it was more than an oversight. We haven't found the person who pulled the alarm." Steve shook his head in disbelief.

"I'm going to get a complex if it keeps up." She wrapped her arms around her middle, wandering tentatively through the small house.

She felt Steve's hand on her shoulder and he pulled her close. "Did you call Fred this morning to let him know we had a snow day?"

Tori shook her head. "I told him to take time off. I didn't think he'd consider showing up. You can't think he'd do this?" Steve didn't say anything, and Tori shook her head. "Do you?"

Steve shrugged. "When I escorted him out of the building, he made a comment that we couldn't keep him from teaching here, claiming he had tenure."

She rolled her eyes. "I don't think he'd do this. And if he did, he wouldn't have stuck around. Why don't you try to call him. See if he answers."

Tori looked for her local phone directory since she'd left her digital address book at her grandparents'. She picked up the phone. "Never mind. The phone's dead."

Luis gave her a panicked look. "Tori, don't touch

anything. I know your fingerprints are already here, but you may smudge any others." She set the phone down with her fingertips.

"Sorry."

"If her phone is dead," Steve said as he turned and looked outside, "shouldn't her grandparents' phone be dead also? If it was knocked out by the storm, that is."

"Makes sense. I'll look to see if it's been cut, but for now, I want you both out of here. I'm locking the house up and we'll get investigators in here as soon as this storm allows."

"What if he comes back?" Tori looked around. "And I'm guessing I won't be living here for a while."

"Afraid not." Luis said, shaking his head. "We'll do what we can to make sure it's secure, but we don't have any extra men. With this storm, we'll have more emergency calls than usual. Unfortunately, that's a major drawback of a small community."

"Is there anyone we could hire to provide security? Someone from Trinidad, maybe?"

"I've got a call in to the sheriff's office for assistance. We'll have to see if they can spare an officer. In the meantime, I'll finish taking pictures inside and out. I'll be down to take a statement from you as soon as I can."

"Can I get a few things?"

"Let's wait, see if CBI comes today. I'd rather they handle it from here, and they are pretty specific about not touching the crime scene." Luis's fat face melted into a sympathetic smile.

Tori looked around one more time, terrified that anyone could hate her enough to do this. "I want to go to the school, see what I can do to clean that up."

"I'll be right there to get pictures of the tire tracks. That's about all we have to go on. The note was typed, so…"

"Note? You didn't tell me there was a note," Tori said, spinning around to see Steve's reaction. "So what did it say?"

Steve's expression was grim and he glanced at Luis, who nodded. "'I know where you live.'"

"That's all?" Tori looked from Luis, back to Steve.

His brows furrowed. "There was a little name-calling."

Something in his expression struck her funny, and she laughed. "Name-calling. And you're not going to tell me what he called me? Luis?"

Luis went back into the house and Steve shook his head. He took hold of her arm and led the way down the street. "I don't think it matters at this point. And this isn't funny."

"Of course not, but being called names isn't anything new."

"I don't repeat these words, and right now, you don't need to hear them. Why don't we stop by your grandparents', let them know what's going on?"

"What about Kelsey and Kyle?"

They're going to hear about it sooner or later. I'd just as soon they hear the truth from us."

She looked at him, startled.

"What?"

She laughed again. "That sounded so…parental."

"I'm entitled."

She looked into his eyes, seeing a reflection of the feelings she, too, was fighting. "Not paternal, parental, together. Struck me funny."

"So there's hope?"

"It's early. I'm just relieved that no one stayed here last night."

They stayed at her grandparents' long enough for Steve and *Abuelo* to fix breakfast and Tori to help *Abuela* with her shower. Afterward, they found a piece of wood large enough to cover the window and Steve took it to the school and nailed it in place.

Tori spent some time moving her books and papers from the wet snow that had blown into her office.

Just before 8:00 a.m., Fred drove up to the school in his four-wheel-drive pickup.

Steve met Fred at the door. "I don't think you should be here, Fred."

"I'm not here to cause any more trouble. I'm here to pack my personal belongings."

Tori stepped into the hall. "Morning." She looked at his pickup and realized he couldn't be responsible for the rock through the school window, his tire tracks were far too big. The culprit's tire tracks were more in keeping with those of a small car, but how it had maneuvered in the deep snow she couldn't figure out.

"I don't have any good excuse for my behavior yesterday. And I'm sorry for the scene in your office, Victoria." He looked at the floor like a beaten child. "I hoped I could weather my last three years to full retirement, but—" he paused, not looking at either Tori or Steve, but the building and trophy case "—times are changing, and I think those changes will go smoother without me here."

"I'm sorry it came to this, Mr. Esquival." Tori was genuinely sorry. "You devoted a lot to this school and the students over the years."

He nodded, tears in his eyes. "Don't mean to sound like a hypocrite, Victoria, but even though I couldn't work for you, I think you'll do a good job here. Steve, good luck. I'd better get my things out of the new teacher's way."

"Thank you, Fred," Steve offered his hand, and the two men shook.

"No need dragging this out any more than necessary…." He handed Tori an envelope. "Here's my resignation. Keys to the school are inside. I suppose the letter should go to the board."

Tori took the envelope and let her hand drop to her side. The past two days had been overwhelming. She hadn't seen this coming.

Steve offered to check him out of the classroom, signing off on the paperwork, and Tori welcomed his intervention. After Fred finished loading his truck, she and Steve returned to her grandparents', finding Kelsey, Kyle and *Abuela* playing a rousing board game.

"*Abuela* keeps taking my marbles!" Kyle complained.

"It's just a game," Kelsey said. "You'll get better, Kyle."

Tori sat down and pulled Kyle into her lap. "We'll show *Abuela* how we really play." Within two rounds, Kyle was well on his way home, and had apprehended two of *Abuela*'s prized marbles.

"Tori has always been the board game champion," *Abuela* told Kyle. "She used to love snow days."

"I still do," Tori insisted.

"And she's apparently still the champion." Steve teased.

Abuela laughed. "I think you have her figured out, Steve."

"Hey, you two, I've had a rough enough day without assessing my game-playing skills," hoping the full meaning of her statement went unnoticed by Kelsey and Kyle.

Steve swiped his hand over his head, motioning that they hadn't understood. "Since I'm not appreciated here, I'll go shovel the walks. Then we should head home. Kids, as soon as you're done with this game, would you get bundled up and come on out? Tori, think the football game will go on as scheduled tomorrow?"

"I called the athletic director from the school. So far, they haven't had more than a skiff of snow in Widefield, so we're still on, as long as the highway department clears our roads before tomorrow morning."

"Are you still planning to go?"

"I still have a condo to rent, so if you'd like to stay here, that's fine."

"It's on my schedule. Just wanted to let Aunt Elaine know the plan. Mr. and Mrs. Sandoval, thank you very much for your hospitality. It was much nicer than throwing sleeping bags on the gym floor like we did during that storm last winter."

"It was a pleasure having company, and thank you for those delicious steaks."

Steve and the kids left soon after that and Tori spent the majority of the afternoon on the phone with her insurance agent and members of the school board. She washed the sheets so they'd be ready for her to stay here a few more nights, then drove to the market and picked up a few things to tide them through the next day while she was gone.

Abuelo looked outside. "Sure appreciate Steve clearing the walks for us."

Tori nodded as she moved the sheets from the washer into the dryer. "He's very thoughtful."

"He's very protective of you. Do you think you're fooling anyone with this co-worker act?"

She froze. "It's not an act. Though we care for each other, *Abuelo,* he wants to raise his children here. And my move here is only temporary. Jerry will be back in a few months, and I'll move back home."

"You think so, do you?"

She wondered if he'd heard something or was merely hoping. "I'm planning on it. Do you know otherwise?"

"You've always had big dreams, Victoria. And you've made sure nothing stands in the way of getting them. I'd just like you to realize God has dreams for you, too. And when I see you and those kids of Steve's together, I think God's hand is at work."

Tori bowed her head and remained in an attitude of frozen stillness.

"I love you like you were my own daughter, angel, but you're a bit strong-willed, and well…some men are frightened away by that. Steve isn't one of those men."

She leaned forward and kissed his cheek. "Thanks for the advice, *Abuelo,* but I can't pretend to be something I'm not. If God had wanted me to be meek and submissive, He wouldn't have given me the gifts and dreams to go into school administration. And I'm sure you're right. It's probably frightened off the wrong men more than once. But that's okay, because I only want the right man to stand by me, like you and *Abuela,* and Mama and Daddy. And in the meantime, I'm keeping busy."

"Maybe too busy. Who needs so many classes? You're doing just fine without more school."

She'd never get them to understand how important education was to her. "I like learning, *Abuelito.*" She added the endearment to his name to let him know she admired him. "It's important to me. And I'm close to finishing."

"We've heard that one before," he mumbled.

The day had gone quickly, and to her surprise, a team of CBI agents arrived later that day to process the break-ins. She wasn't sure how she convinced her grandfather to stay home when she went over to answer their questions, but she was very thankful he did. She didn't want him to be afraid to have her living there alone after the mess was cleaned up. Her own fears she could deal with, but his, she wasn't so sure about.

Chapter Twelve

Saturday morning Tori and Steve followed the bus to the game. They watched the team rally to victory behind the leadership of Tommy Jiminez, cousin of the student who stabbed Marcus Tiponi. She wondered if Tommy and Miguel were close, and if Tommy also held a grudge against her for expelling his cousin from school. One challenge of the predominantly Hispanic community was the unbreakable dedication to taking care of family. That instinct was as strong as that of a mother bear with her cubs, and if broken, equally as dangerous for the predator.

She and Steve visited with the parents of the players while they waited for the kids to board the bus. She held her breath when she saw Tommy headed in her direction.

"Hey, Miz Sandoval," Tommy said. "Thanks for coming to the game."

"Congratulations on a great game, Tommy." The

hometown crowd cheered as the rest of the team came out of the locker room, and Tommy leaned closer. "Sorry about my cousin." Tommy shrugged with an arrogance that she was all too familiar with from the gangs in the city. "What can I say, but Miguel's messed up, man. My aunt, well, she let him bully everyone since we's little. Stupid bum will probably end up in jail if they find him again, won't he?"

"I'm not sure, Tommy, but thanks for letting me know where you stand."

"I heard about your house. If you need help fixing it up, let me know. I painted houses last summer for extra money. But I wouldn't charge you."

"Jiminez, let's go!" Coach Hunt called from the bus, waving to Tori.

"Have a good weekend, Tommy."

Steve kept a respectable distance as they walked to her SUV. "What was that about?"

"He apologized for Miguel's actions. Sounds like he thinks it was Miguel that tore apart my house."

"I thought he was in jail at the time it happened."

She unlocked the doors and they slipped inside. "Luis came by last night with the investigators. His mother couldn't post bail, but his dad did by wire from Texas. So now they think that Miguel trashed my house. They haven't found him yet, but they've sent out an all-points bulletin for his arrest. Since he ran, and it's not his first felony charge, I doubt he'll get another chance at bail."

"So it's not over?"

"Not yet, but soon I hope. Let's talk about something more pleasant, like maybe I'll rent my condo today." She turned out of Widefield and headed north into Colorado Springs.

"Do you miss the city as much as you thought you would?"

"Yes," she said simply and honestly. "But like I expected, Segundo has its benefits."

He raised his eyebrows. "Even this week, with all that went wrong?"

"Even through all that, God let me see the good side of going home. This could have happened at any school." She reached for the gearshift of her manual transmission and Steve placed his hand on hers. "Sounds like you're growing used to taking those risks."

"I'm going to have to. We haven't even launched our night school program idea yet."

"I have to admit, I was more than a little surprised at the amount of interest shown in night classes. I hope it goes so well they offer a full schedule next year."

Tori laughed. "You're already starting to sound like a hopeful administrator. For the record, I think it's worth looking into. Colorado Springs High has a booming program with their night school. If you'd like me to get you a name to contact, I'd be happy to."

"I'd appreciate it." The radio filled the silence until Steve thought of another subject. "You didn't happen to find any new clues to who pulled the fire alarm, did you?"

She shook her head and moved her hand back to the steering wheel. "I can't help but wonder if that could have been Fred, too. He seemed pretty intent on us punishing a culprit."

Steve lifted his hands in bewilderment. "Who knows? He could have, I suppose. I couldn't believe he was the same man this week as the man I met last year."

"Was he different before they hired me, or did the change start once I arrived on the picture?"

Steve shrugged and Tori sensed his reluctance to answer. "A little different before, but more what I thought of as nervous about the tenuous situation at the school overall. Jerry wasn't here at all, there was talk about closing the school immediately, and then your name came up."

"So I take it that was your idea?"

"Not really," Steve said, vehemently shaking his head. "No, I don't think so. It was Jerry's idea all the way." No matter how defensive Steve became, she still suspected he had at least planted the seed in Jerry's mind. She felt her heart swell knowing that he'd wanted her here badly enough to sacrifice their personal relationship.

Tori pulled into the driveway and turned off the engine. "Well," she said looking at her watch, "they should be here soon. I called them while you were in the locker room with the team. Let's go in and make sure the cleaning company lives up to their reputation."

She led the way inside remembering how she and Steve fought the last time they were here together. "Why didn't you just tell me from the beginning that you were the administrative intern?"

He closed the door and took his coat off. "Because I was afraid you'd turn the job down, and that you'd choose to stay here in this house that's as beautiful as you deserve. Because I wanted a chance to get to know each other better without scaring you away by telling you how much I care for you."

She laughed, then, seeing the disappointment in Steve's eyes, she realized she hadn't registered the significance of his words. "So instead, I'm just plain scared." Tori walked up the stairs backward. "Come on. You may as well get the full tour."

He followed, glancing in the empty rooms. While she inspected each one, he waited on the balcony, looking out the windows at the view of the Black Forest region in the distance.

"You had a beautiful view. I'm sorry, Tori. I never dreamed you'd be in danger coming home."

Tori leaned against the rail next to him. "Only danger I expected was losing my heart. Now, I'm afraid of losing my job, my home and you." He reached out to her, but she slipped from his grasp. She went downstairs, then around the corner to the basement stairs.

Steve stayed in the living room and continued the conversation when she joined him again. "Why do you think that?" He took her hand as she headed for the kitchen and didn't let go this time. He pulled her to face him. "The inspection can wait a minute."

"Even my own grandfather says I'm too strong-willed to keep a good man. I should be more vulnerable, or submissive, or…" She shrugged herself away from his gentle hold.

"That's not true."

"And pretending that I'm not interested in you is about to kill me. I have no way of knowing if *Abuelo*'s right or not. Besides, I'm a terrible actress. Even Carly's noticed the electricity when we're in the same room."

"I happen to love strong women, especially one prone to telling the truth and doing the right thing even when it isn't the easiest thing to do. Don't worry. You're quite a catch just as you are. Maybe if I were a little more noble, I'd offer to drop my internship." Steve took her in his arms, and she lifted her chin.

"Are you offering?" she asked as his lips gently touched hers.

The doorbell rang, jolting them apart like a bolt of lightning. Tori's heart raced and she ran into the wall, collapsing with laughter. "God's not even going to let us sneak in one kiss, is He?"

Steve wasn't laughing. "Guess we have our answer to the ultimate question. He doesn't want to make liars of us." He strolled forward and extended a hand, pulling her to her feet. "Since it's your house, it'd probably look better if you answer."

Tori opened the door, welcoming the young couple in. She introduced Steve as a co-worker, explaining that they'd come to the football game together. She could barely tell the truth without feeling guilty anymore.

After she'd given them a tour, she reminded them of the price and the terms of the lease. "Since I've already checked your references, you have the advantage," she told them. "If you're interested, I'd love to have you as tenants."

"We're very interested, and it's even prettier than we expected. Kevin told us about your grandmother. How's she doing?" the wife asked.

Tori smiled. "Very well. She's getting herself around, and I wouldn't doubt it if she starts walking again. But don't worry, I don't think there's a chance of me coming back before summer in any case."

The couple looked at each other with concern. "We have one complication. I just found out that we're pregnant. Since I've already lost a baby in the last trimester, the doctor told me to plan to go on bed rest in April. Moving would be out of the question until at least August."

"Congratulations. You must be thrilled." She glanced at Steve whose expression was as unreadable as it had been after the doorbell rang. "I'm sure I can work around that, if necessary."

"And if you decide not to come back, are kids okay?"

Tori looked at the husband, blank. She had no idea if the association had any regulations against children.

"In the condo, I mean."

"I'm sure this sounds stupid, but I'm not sure. In a

four-bedroom condo, you'd think so, wouldn't you? I wasn't able to get my paperwork from my files before I left today, but I'll look and make sure."

"Do any of the neighbors have kids?" Steve asked.

Tori shrugged. "Not that I can think of, but that doesn't say much. I'm not outside much to notice."

After giving the couple a tentative agreement on a handshake, Tori and Steve left to go see Jerry. Steve was unusually quiet. Since Jerry was back in intensive care, they gave him a quick update and left without any of the advice they had hoped to receive.

"Want to stop for dinner?" She hoped they could finish their conversation over a cozy table for two.

"Sure."

When she pulled into the restaurant Steve seemed surprised. "Are we dressed appropriately?"

"We're fine. You do like Chinese food, don't you?"

"Sure."

She looked at him. "You don't sound too excited. We can go someplace else if you'd like. I picked this because we don't have any really good Oriental food in the valley."

"At least you thought this decision out carefully," Steve said as he opened the door.

Despite her confusion about his comment, she went on inside and asked for a table for two.

"Corner table okay?" the hostess asked.

Tori looked at Steve and nodded. "Fine."

Steve followed, sat down next to her and began reading the menu without a word.

"So what does that remark mean? What did I do wrong?"

His answer was delayed by the waitress taking their order. "Would you like saki or wine?"

"No," they said together.

What she'd hoped to be a cozy table for two ended up being a crowded table of aggravation. "How could you not know if you're buying into a place that allows children? And you don't even know if there are kids in the complex?"

She stared at him. "I'm sorry. Kids weren't in my foreseeable future."

He backed away and she could almost feel his body tense. "You're around kids every day. Which leads me to believe you're either sick of them by the time you get home, or you chose not to make room in your busy life for them."

She felt as if the spotlight had just shone on them as their appetizer platter with the tiny grill arrived and the guests looked at them with envy. Tori tried to act natural, but the sizzling meat continued to draw unwelcome attention.

"Neither is true," she whispered. "Not exactly, anyway. I didn't think I'd have kids because I don't date much."

Steve moved closer until Tori had no room at all. "What? I couldn't hear that last part."

She repeated herself and he laughed. "Right."

"I didn't have time. It was a larger school and I was even busier than I am now." She nibbled the teriyaki beef from the stick.

"So your career comes first."

"I'd rather not argue about this with an audience, if you don't mind." The rest of the dinner was a hurried blur to get out of the tight quarters. Steve insisted on paying the bill, and Tori didn't argue. She felt sure that their discussion was far from over.

When Steve got into the SUV he pulled the parking brake, stopping her from leaving. "If this is the only chance we're going to have to be alone, I'd like to take advantage of it. We need to talk."

"I'm not discussing children in a parking lot!"

His laughter rolled from deep in his chest. "What's wrong with it? No one can hear us in here."

"These are the same people leaving the restaurant that were watching us argue inside." Tori pushed his hand off the brake and backed out. "There's a park not too far from here if you insist that we can't discuss it while we drive."

"Sounds good to me. Safety first, and it seems to be a volatile subject."

She drove for a few blocks to a wooded park and pulled to a stop, leaving the engine running. "What is so absurd about not noticing kids in my neighborhood? I generally get home after dark when well-supervised children are inside."

"Most women—" He turned in his seat to face her. "Not that you have to be like most women, but generally speaking, an attractive woman such as yourself would be beating men off with a stick. And somewhere along the way, women at least think about children, if not—"

"Feel the biological clock ticking?" she finished.

"Doesn't that concern you? Or did you never want kids?"

"Of course I wanted children, but not without a father and a happy marriage. Sounds like you've been talking to Brody."

"A little."

She felt the walls close in around her. "Do you want to know about Brody and I specifically, or me and men in general?"

"Wherever you want to start."

She took a deep breath and closed her eyes. "The only realistic future for girls like me was to marry a rich rancher or have babies. And to some extent, the latter was a very popular choice, starting in high school. I was tired of seeing doors close in my face because of the color of my skin. I was determined not to fall into that category. I wanted to make something of myself first, to break the stereotype. So after graduation I broke it off with Brody because I knew his future was there at the ranch."

"Is that so bad?"

"It was at the time. Elaine and Bill are wonderful, and I loved Brody, as much as a teenager knows about love. But my parents thought of them as *Abuela*'s boss. And it wasn't at all right for me to marry out of our class. If they had their way I'd marry a missionary and have lots of babies—even now."

"Didn't they leave your grandparents to raise you while they went out of the country?"

"Oh, that didn't matter. I was with family, and they thought that was the same as if I was with them. So they tried 'parenting' me from across the ocean. In the Hispanic culture, family is second only to God, so leaving me with my grandparents was normal."

"Nothing wrong with the philosophy of God and family, but I know what you mean about being left behind, or being sent away. You miss your parents both ways."

"I have no issue with God and family coming first, don't get me wrong. And I support my parents' mission, now, but at the time, I wanted to be like other families. I wanted my parents to want me. And to them, I stood in the way of their work. So they chose their work over being parents."

"I guess it could have been worse, for both of us."

Tori nodded. "We see proof of that every day. And I still don't like that education is way down the list for families around here."

"That came as quite an eye-opener for me, too. Especially from a family of professionals. Dad was a doctor, and Mom at least had her degree in finance, though she never worked outside the house."

"Yes, I imagine this has been an adjustment for you." Tori's eyes widened. "It's not uncommon for a ten-year-old child to be expected to stay home from school to watch the younger siblings while Mom and Dad are out working or…whatever. I saw friends whose mothers kept having kids even though they couldn't afford to feed them. They'd send one or two children to the grandparents' house and have another baby. Eventually, kids were the ones having the babies, dropping out of school, starting the cycle all over again. I can't change the world, but I wasn't about to keep the cycle going. Luckily, Brody and I both felt strongly about education and waiting for marriage. So I stuck my nose in the books, and after I went to college, I vowed to wait until I had my diploma before I even tempted myself to date again."

"I'm sure Brody would have encouraged your studies. Why didn't you ask him to wait for you to finish?"

"Because I didn't want to argue with my parents for the rest of my life. Once I was away, I didn't want to come back. I never would have if it hadn't been for Grandmother's stroke."

"Did you still love Brody, after college?"

"It was a comfortable, safe first love. When I look back, it was more like best friends. He was devoted to sports, and I to my grades. Mrs. Primrose thought I was brilliant and told me I could go to college on a scholarship if I kept my grades up, and she was right. My parents didn't see the value of an education and couldn't understand me going into teaching.

"After college I spent every spare minute preparing my classes and grading labs. I dated some, but never met anyone who kept my attention. Then I went back to school for my master's degree, and somewhere along the way, I realized that what *Abuelo* said today is pretty true. A lot of men are intimidated by a take-charge woman."

"Not all men," Steve confessed. "And it doesn't mean there's anything wrong with being who you are."

"Thanks. The schedule of an administrator isn't too dating-friendly, either, in case you're seriously considering that as your new career. And some teachers' spouses resent students getting more of their spouse's attention than their own kids. One administrator, whom I knew, lived with her boyfriend. One day he told her he'd been dating someone else for a year. She'd been so busy she hadn't even realized it. He was married three months later. She's still married to her school." Tori laughed. "I realized tonight when Dustin asked if kids are permitted, that I've been just as blind.

"It does not mean that I don't want children. I simply wanted to be able to provide for them and be there to raise them myself…without grandparents or boarding schools. I know my priorities would need to change. Hopefully it's not too late."

"I'm sorry I doubted you." He leaned across the console and shattered the calm with the simple touch of his lips on hers.

She closed her eyes and sent a silent prayer heavenward. *Please, God, let Steve be the one You've kept me waiting for.*

Chapter Thirteen

Sunday evening Steve arrived at church late and pushed the kids on past the group gathered at the back of the sanctuary. "Looks like there's room in the pews up front," he told Kyle as he looked to see the reason for the commotion. Immediately he found Tori and understood. Tonight warranted a welcome-back for her grandparents, and their friends were glad to oblige.

He hadn't seen them in church since Maria's stroke. Steve offered a smile, hurrying to get the kids settled, when the organist began the prelude.

Since their drive home from Colorado Springs, he'd been thinking a lot about Tori. They had talked about God and church, and he wondered if she was here today because of their conversation. They had a lot in common, from opposite ends of the spectrum. They'd both been raised away from their parents, they were both determined and had never given up on their dreams. They both admitted to taking on more than they should and finding themselves letting a busy schedule take over. They had so much in common it frightened Steve a little. Though a lot of people felt comforted by similarities, Steve had wanted to find a wife whose personality acted as a balance to his own. Instead he'd found another Anna.

Both were beautiful, but in very different ways. Tori was bronzed and breathtaking; Anna had been blonde and bodacious. Yet both were intelligent, confident and devoted to their careers.

I came out here to find a slower pace, Lord. I wanted to find a woman whose top priority would be family, one who isn't obsessed with her career. A woman who can help me teach Kelsey and Kyle about Your miraculous love. If Tori isn't that woman, Lord, keep me from temptation.

Steve couldn't believe his mind had wandered through the announcements, shared praises and into the first hymn. He stood, searching through the hymnal for the selected song. Kelsey nudged him, "Dad, Kyle is making stupid faces and taking my new pen."

"She won't share," Kyle said in retaliation. *Why do they have to act up today, at church?* Steve thought. He tried to be discreet about separating them, but he felt all eyes on him. Kyle stood on the pew and pulled Steve's organizer from his shirt pocket. Before Steve could react, Kyle had already made himself comfortable and found a file of games to play. The woman in the pew behind jabbed Steve's shoulder with her sharp finger and pointed at Kyle as if Steve had been sleeping though the incident. "He should learn to sing the hymns," she scolded.

"He's fine. This keeps him occupied," he whispered back, wondering if she'd ever had children. He looked at the words in the hymnal and wondered if she realized Kyle wasn't even reading multisyllable words, let alone music yet. He was often mistaken for much older than six and Steve wondered if part of the problem was when people saw Steve's hair was more salt than pepper they expected all of them to be older than they looked.

She cleared her throat and Steve succumbed to pressure. He took the game from Kyle and lifted him into his arms. "I know you can't read the music, but you need to at least listen quietly. Okay?"

Kyle groaned softly. "I want to sit in the back where we usually sit."

"Not today. Shhh." Steve set the book down and continued to sing, holding Kyle still.

Kyle eventually calmed down. Just as the hymn ended, Kyle tapped Steve's shoulder. "Dad, I see Tori!" Steve turned, catching a glimpse of Tori smiling and waving to Kyle.

Steve handed Kyle the game again as they sat down. "Here, now play quietly," he whispered. If the woman behind him didn't like it, maybe she'd suggest they have a children's hour so the adults wouldn't be interrupted.

Steve couldn't seem to stay focused today and he tried to get his mind off of Tori. Though he had no doubts about how he felt for her, he did question whether he should have feelings for her at all. Steve even wondered if he would play second fiddle to her first love, Brody. At least last they had settled two issues last night—Brody and children. Not that one discussion erased all of their roadblocks, but if they could jump one issue at a time, they'd have it made. They were a far cry from commitment, but at Steve's age, he wasn't willing to waste his time on the wrong woman. He'd been discussing marriage with God for quite a while and waiting patiently for His answer. Could Tori be the one, or was Steve simply losing his patience?

Steve closed his eyes and listened to the Bible passage from Hebrews. "Do not lose courage, then, because it brings with it a great reward. You need to be patient in order to do the will of God and receive what He promises." Steve couldn't help but feel thankful for God's reassurance. Just seeing Tori here this evening gave him hope that she was not only his choice, but God's also. It had been difficult to approach the dating scene again. After fifteen years with Anna, he'd forgotten what it was like to get to know a woman. And he was quickly losing confidence that he'd find that right partner from the few single women in his age range in the valley. God definitely answered prayers.

The choir sat down and the pastor began the sermon. As always, Pastor Ramon surprised him with how he kept up with the current events in Coal Valley, even though he only traveled up here for church each Sunday. His sermon had obviously been written the night before, as it addressed looking for the blessings in our daily lives amid troubling events. "God doesn't wait for one of His children to come to Him in times of need. He is there with us before we ask. He cares about the scrape on a child's knee as she picks up her bicycle from the blacktop. He cares about the family struggling to make ends meet. He is here to share our every joy and sorrow—" the pastor paused "—with or without invitation. How we see His power to change our outlook is up to us."

He expressed joy for the football team's victory and ability to stay focused after distractions at school during the week. And in his closing prayer he said, "Our thoughts and prayers will be with the Sandoval family this week as Victoria begins cleaning up from the break-in at her house. We ask for His divine protection over the teachers, staff and students attending our schools."

Tori's eyes shimmered when Steve welcomed her to the congregation. "I never quite get over how quickly news travels here," she said.

"I think Pastor Ramon has some divine connections that even bypass the gossip chains."

"I hope not. I'd like to preserve a few secrets." She turned her smile up a notch, and he knew immediately that she was referring to their kiss.

Steve straightened his shoulders and fought to keep a straight face. "Then you'd better develop a better poker face than that."

"I never admitted to being a good actress, and I've never played poker." She somehow managed to clear the admiration from her face with the change of the subject. "Jason Hunt called this afternoon and offered his van to take us all to Pikes Peak High School tomorrow. He said that he'd thought of it before, but there were too many of us. Now that Fred's not going, it should work. I hate to bombard everyone with business on the road, but do you think it's a good time to discuss the attendance policy? Maybe if we can come to an agreement, we could take it to the board meeting tomorrow night."

She never ceased to amaze him with the way she could move from one subject to the next without one hint of transition. "It's Sunday. Take a minute to relax and set work aside, would you?"

"A simple yes or no would end the subject," she said, clearly annoyed with his criticism. He nodded, and again she changed the subject. "So what did you do to relax today?"

"The kids and I just did a little tinkering on the house and watched football." He didn't mention that the house was a mere shell at this point, or that the crew worked like banshees to get the windows and doors finished before the snow flew. He knew he should tell her he didn't plan to live at the ranch forever, that it was a temporary situation, somewhat like hers, but he didn't want her to read anything into the house meaning he was permanently attached to the area. Despite a new house, he'd move in a heartbeat in the right circumstances. "And you? Did you work on cleaning up your place?"

She frowned. "Looked for the contract on my condo, which does allow children, by the way. And I went to the school to retype a lease for the Browns since my computer is dead. What did you think of them? Think I made the right choice?"

"To lease to them? Sure. They seem like a nice couple."

Pastor Ramon stopped by to say goodbye, hinting that they, too, needed to leave.

Steve thought it was strange that a workaholic like Tori hadn't started cleaning anything yet, until the next morning when he walked into her office. He knocked on the glassless oak door and froze. His eyes shot open.

"Morning," Tori said lightly.

He quickly found where she'd spent the majority of her day—cleaning and rearranging her office. "Either you've been here all night, or you spent your Sunday here working." Visions of Anna's court documents spread neatly over their bed came to mind and Steve wondered how he could let himself fall in love with another woman whose drive for success ruled her every waking moment.

Tori disappeared under her desk with the cord to her mouse. "I fixed green chile for Sunday dinner, finished the laundry for all of us and came over here when they fell asleep watching the football game." She reappeared and looked at him with that dark-eyed "don't mess with me" stare. "And I even followed your suggestion to relax for a few minutes when I fell asleep reading the covenant to my condo."

She sat in the chair, testing the range of motion of the newly affixed control to her computer. "There, that's better."

"So you don't mind living in a mess, but you have to have order to your office?" He studied the interesting arrangement, and she studied him.

"Sitting with my back to the window—" she motioned to the wooden patch "—when there is a window, gives me the chills after the break-in. I'd just as soon be able to see who's watching me, if you don't mind. Besides, it'll nice to see what's going on at my grandparents' and in the parking lot."

Through all of this, she'd remained eerily calm. "You can't control every bit of your life, Tori."

She hit the print button on her computer and walked to the printer in the outer office. "Carly is going to come in today to meet the repairmen. They should be able to have the window replaced by this evening. When the kids come tomorrow morning, all that will be left of the incident is a bad memory and a new substitute. The board votes tonight on whether to approve Fred's resignation. We should be there."

He shook his head and sat in the chair across from her desk. "I'm planning on it." He waited fruitlessly for her to respond to his comment. He leaned forward, resting his elbows on his knees. Steve lowered his voice so anyone who happened into the office couldn't hear. "Stress has a way of finding a way out of our bodies, Tori. Anna's illness was evidence of that, and I don't plan to watch another woman I love let her job kill her."

"Then maybe you shouldn't have brought me here," she said quietly. "I do the job the best way I know how, with my whole heart. Organization is my stress-buster, and once I have the school back in order, I'll move on to my house. Until the insurance adjuster comes to file the claim, I can't do anything. Is there anything else you'd like to change about me this morning?"

The sound of cars driving on the ice outside broke the tension in the room. "I'm just concerned about you. I'll be in my classroom working. Give me a call when you're ready to leave."

Steve went to his classroom and went through the steps of putting up a new bulletin board. Themes for high school math tended to be hard to come by, so he'd invited students to earn extra credit for every news article they could find where math played a role. With the recent space exploration, he'd been deluged with articles, forcing him to remove the outdated information from one board to make room for more submissions.

He had underestimated student's interest in the high-tech world outside their environment. He had reports of not only NASA's projects, but also on computers and science. The one that surprised him most had actually been written by Corey Claiborne, formatted in newspaper columns no less, based upon a documentary he'd watched on the History Channel on the high-tech methods of sniper weaponry used by the army. Steve had questioned whether to accept it, since it wasn't a real news clipping, so he dug through the cable guide until he found the next showing. The facts were flawless. Corey's interests were diverse—art, science, military weaponry. And who knew where else his curiosity would take him. What concerned Steve was Corey's reclusive personality.

He pinned the article to the board, making note to ask if other teachers would be interested in suggesting students write reviews of television programs as a way to generate more interest in writing.

"We're ready to go, Larisa." Steve heard Tori's voice down the hall as she worked her way closer, stopping at each classroom. He'd expected her to make an announcement over the intercom, not walk the halls.

"Steve, we're ready to go," she said, and spun away.

He set the folder of clippings on his desk and turned out the light, hurrying to catch up with her. Larisa Matheson and Tracy Hayes were way ahead of them, though Tori didn't seem to be trying to catch up to them.

Gone was Tori's frumpy suit, he noticed. This lucky day she wore a purple knit dress and leather boots that kept his eyes locked on her like radar. "Something wrong with the intercom, or did you just want a walk before we spend the day sitting?"

She turned, but didn't stop walking. "As a matter of fact, there is a problem with the intercom. The microphone has no on/off switch. It has been removed since Thursday morning's announcements were made. You figure that one out."

He picked up the pace, "That was one strange day."

"I'm going to suggest we hire a campus monitor. This has got to stop. No wonder Jerry got sick, trying to be superintendent, principal and security simultaneously."

"Do you think the same person who broke into your house would have done it?"

"Taken the buttons from the intercom? They didn't touch the computers, the copiers or even the lunch money box in the file, but they took the buttons from the intercom?" She had that "in-charge" glow to her this morning. Maybe she did find organizing things relaxing. More power to her.

Maybe God had brought her into his life to lift that burden from his own shoulders. Maybe Steve was the one who needed to change. She turned into the office, slipped on her coat and picked up her briefcase. Steve grabbed his coat and bag from the chair and followed her outside.

Tori paused as the van's sliding door opened automatically. Jason motioned to the back. "Looks like you two get the jump seat."

Daria was up front with Jason, which startled Steve. He'd done all he could to shake her since the day he'd walked into the school, and suddenly, she was giving up? Angelia got out of the seat next to the door and popped her seat forward so Tori and Steve could climb into the back.

"Nice van, Jason. Has all the bells and whistles," Steve said, hoping to take the attention off him as Tori climbed in. He counted heads. "Isn't Geoff coming?"

"We're picking him up on our way through Trinidad."

"Good plan."

Though it was nice to have everyone together, Steve missed the leg room of his truck. Tori seemed to notice, too, as she repeatedly tugged the hem of her dress over her knees. Finally she plopped her briefcase onto her lap and pulled out the agenda for this week's staff meeting. "Would anyone mind if we take care of our staff meeting while we drive?"

It was unanimously approved.

"We haven't had much opportunity to address the goals we made when I first arrived, plus, I'd like to take the proposed attendance policy to the board meeting tonight." She quickly updated them all on Fred's resignation and the break-in at her house, asking anyone who heard anything about Miguel's location to contact the sheriff. "Larisa, if you can hear everyone okay from up there, would you mind holding a recorder so we'll have notes of the meeting?" She gave the small hand-held cassette recorder to the teacher in front of her.

The discussion went well, and the teachers voted overwhelmingly to recommend adding an additional fifteen minutes to each day in order to make up for the additional week off in the spring.

They stopped at the college on their way into town and Tracy moved to the back. Steve scooted to the middle of the bench seat, forced to cozy up either to Tori or the pregnant teacher to his right. His shoulders simply didn't fit well with Tori trying to take notes. He tried tucking his hands next to his legs, but when his hand brushed her leg, it made Tori nearly hit her head on the roof, and everyone laughed. "Excuse me," he said, biting the bullet as he rested his arm on the seat behind her, bringing the dreaded razzing from everyone. He felt Tori's back stiffen, and he had to do something to make light of the situation or risk her reaction telling the truth. He leaned over and gave her an exaggerated kiss on her cheek. "A man's gotta do what a man's gotta do."

"Well, Mr. Remington, I never!" she said in a sultry Southern accent.

"Write him up for a PDA!"

Steve laughed, and so did everyone else, even as the rest of them threw out the suggestion to report Steve for the "public display of affection' since they weren't on school campus.

After they settled down, Tori kept everyone involved as she went down the list of goals they had made at their first meeting.

She struggled to ignore the fact that she and Steve were snug as two bugs in a rug, with all of their peers as an audience.

They arrived at the school just before ten. The staff of Tori's school were just beginning to gather for the in-service training. Out of nowhere a good-looking football-player-built guy wrapped his arm around Tori's shoulder and said, "Hey, there, Squeaky, we miss you around here."

"Squeaky?" Tori made no move to escape. Of course,

from Steve's estimation, one wrong move and the guy could break her neck with his pinky. She went into the auditorium wrapped in his embrace. "Squeaky's here!" The big guy bellowed and the noise hit deafening levels.

The principal introduced the staff from Coal Valley and reviewed the plans for the mentor program. Kevin explained what they were hoping to accomplish this year and asked that the different subject areas break off for discussion of literacy goals. After they broke for lunch, they met briefly for an overview of what had worked in the larger school. Several ideas actually lent themselves better to the smaller environment at Coal Valley, if they could get and keep parents involved.

Somehow Tori and Steve were, again, the last two to the van, and though they didn't end up in the back seat, they did end up side by side. Steve certainly didn't mind, but the tension seemed to take its toll on Tori. Daria ribbed Tori about the football player. "So, Squeaky, you going to tell us where the pet name came from, or do we get to guess?"

"Don't get carried away with ideas. He's called me that because, even in college, he couldn't get me to break the rules. It's short for 'squeaky clean,' but feel free to continue calling me Tori. Really."

Chapter Fourteen

Homecoming week started out with an unexpected surprise when Tori called Marcus's sister into the office. "Nicole, I understand Marcus and Miguel's disagreement had something to do with you dating Miguel."

The pretty senior nodded.

"Marcus seems very concerned. Why do you think Marcus is upset about you and Miguel?" Tori wanted to stop any problems before they had a chance to start. She would ask about her numerous absences later.

Nicole shifted in the chair and looked at her hands. "They just don't like each other."

"They've gone to school since they were in kindergarten and according to their discipline records, they've never fought before. What happened? Has Miguel hurt you?"

"Now you sound like Marcus. He walked in on us at the house one day and thinks he has to be boss."

"Nicole, your brother's concerned about you. I understand your mother's been trying to work a second job to make things a little easier for all of you, and being the oldest boy in the family, Marcus feels responsible to watch over the rest of you."

Nicole argued that she was the oldest, and she could take care of herself. Tori asked a few more questions and was about to ask why she'd been missing so much school when Nicole burst into tears. "I'm not ever going to see Miguel again, anyway."

Tori handed her a tissue. "Do you want to keep seeing him?"

"You don't understand, Miz Sandoval."

Tori wondered if she'd done the right thing bringing Nicole in to talk. Maybe things would have blown over now that Miguel had run off. "I want to understand, Nicole. And if there's anything I can do to help, let me know."

Nicole muttered something in Spanish about a *niña,* and Tori's heart stopped. "What did you say?"

"I said I'm not a baby."

"I didn't say you are. You have a future ahead of you, Nicole. There are a lot of big decisions ahead, and it's important that you make wise choices, from friends, to school, to…"

"Sex?" Nicole said with tears in her eyes.

Tori stepped from around her desk and closed the new shade covering the window on her door. She sat in the chair next to Nicole. "Especially about that. There is a lot of responsibility that comes with intimacy, and a lot of danger that can result from going into an intimate relationship without careful consideration."

"Miguel said he loved me. And that he would take care of things."

She wanted to tell Nicole the truth about teenagers and love, that Nicole didn't have to prove her feelings for anyone through sex, but Nicole's tears told her it was already too late. As much as Tori hated having this conversation, she had to ask some very difficult questions. She wasn't surprised by the answers, but very disappointed.

"You have to tell your mother, Nicole."

"I'll be eighteen soon, and I don't have to tell her I'm pregnant. Besides, Miguel was going to take me to a doctor…." She started crying again. "I can't go to college with a baby…."

Tori wanted to scream, to cry and to give Nicole the motherly love she needed right now. Instead she reached her hand toward Nicole, and welcomed the petite teenager into her embrace. "Nicole, two wrongs don't make a right. This baby is growing now, and you won't ever forget about it. I know it's frightening, but this is not a decision you can make quickly or without counseling."

"Mom said I can't go to school if I have a baby. She said nothin's as good after you have kids. And she said if I get pregnant, I can't live at home, either. She hates me."

Tori held her tight. "No, no, no, Nicole. That's not true. It sounds like maybe your mother was trying to scare you away from being careless, or in this case, to be careful of the friends you choose. It doesn't mean she doesn't love you."

"She warned me to stay away from him. She just yells at me to stop seeing him. She doesn't listen to me."

Tori looked her in the eye. "I'm listening, and I'm sure that your mother will, too. Your mother came in last week to talk with us about the fight. I know how much she worries about you and Marcus and your sisters."

"And now look what a mess I'm in. I didn't think…" She lowered her head and cried. "I just want this to go away. I want to forget Miguel and finish school and let things be the same as they were…."

"Nothing will ever be the same. But it doesn't mean life can't be as good. A child is a huge responsibility, but there are a lot of options for young mothers now. Aborting the baby…" The words stuck in her throat, the words she was supposed to say professionally, but couldn't morally say. Abortion was legally an option with parental consent, but she wouldn't encourage it, even if the board fired her. Not after losing her friend to complications from having one. Not with her belief in God as the Creator. "It isn't easy, physically or emotionally. You must get counseling with someone who can help you make this decision—your mother, your pastor, your doc…"

Nicole interrupted her again, and Tori wondered if Nicole had heard anything Tori had said. "Have you had one, Miss Sandoval?"

"One what?"

"Abortion. You sound like you know all about it."

"No, I haven't," she said. "When I was in school here, a friend of mine had one. There are a lot of risks, Nicole. I read a lot of stories about women who had abortions and how sorry they are. It's not as easy as it sounds."

"Do you believe in God, Miss Sandoval?"

"Yes, I do. Since you asked, I also believe God allowed you to conceive this child for a special reason. You should talk to Him about your decision. He may even have some ideas you haven't thought about. Some that your mother may be happy with, too."

"I don't want to tell my mom yet, but when I do, would you come with me?"

Tori couldn't say no. She felt responsible to make sure Nicole stayed safe, whether it be from a violent boyfriend or an upset mother. "Sure. Come in tomorrow and we'll schedule a meeting with her, okay?"

"Tomorrow?"

"You'll need medical attention soon, and if you're feeling sick, your mom will need to know why. You've been missing a lot of classes. Is that why?"

She nodded.

"Be sure to take good care of yourself and eat right. And for the record, we don't kick you out of school when you're pregnant. Your education is very important to your future. Lots of mothers go to college these days."

Though Tori thought their conversation was nearing

an end, they talked for another hour about college hopes and dreams. Tori hoped she had given Nicole the right advice.

When Nicole left the office, Steve and Carly were at the front desk. Once they could see Nicole cross the parking lot, Steve followed Tori into her office and closed the door.

"Are you okay?"

"No, I'm not," she said, pulling a file from the drawer.

"Is Nicole okay?"

Tori set the file of blank reports on the desk and sat behind the desk. "Depends on your perspective, I guess. If a happily married woman were in Nicole's shoes, she would probably be feeling very okay right now. But this is a seventeen-year-old who thinks her life is over."

"You sure she's okay to walk home by herself in this shape?"

"I have to trust she will take my advice and be back here tomorrow for a meeting with her mother."

Tori felt moisture avalanche down the bridge of her nose, while Steve waited patiently for her to say more.

"Does this have anything to do with the fight?"

Tori nodded. She dug through the olive-wood pencil holder that her parents had brought her from Israel, searching for the fine-tip black pen.

"Could we have stopped anything from happening by doing anything different?"

She shook her head. "It was done by the time we

were involved." Tori turned her attention to filling out paperwork, wishing there were more she could do. "She wants to end the pregnancy."

"Oh." Steve walked around the desk and knelt next to the chair, turning it toward him. "That's a difficult thing to hear."

She took one look at Steve and felt her strength vanish. "She wants to go to college."

"She's talking to the right woman for encouragement," he said. "You came here to make a difference, Tori, and God has opened all kinds of doors to let you do that, but you can't shoulder the blame for kids being human. Maybe you never made bad choices, but I sure did, and I even expect my kids will make a few as time goes by." He smiled, and Tori let him pull her into his embrace for a moment. "I love the way you care for these kids and give them every ounce of attention that you can."

"But?" She leaned her elbows on her knees and rested her forehead against his.

"But nothing. You seem to feel what these kids are feeling. That's why you're a great addition to the school." His thumbs brushed the back of her hand. "These kids need to know their principal cares, and you're making a great impression on them."

"I hope so. If we don't make sure that their basic needs have been met, we can't begin to teach them. I'd like to start a parent support group, kind of a slant off of the old parent-teacher organiz—"

Steve planted a quick kiss on her mouth, enticing her

to set aside their professional discussion. For a moment she forgot that they were here as professionals and let emotion fill her heart.

She regained her strength little by little, breaking the kiss, taking her hand off Steve's neck and finally, pressing her back to the chair. It seemed to jolt her into reality. "Much as I appreciate your comfort, Steve, I think you'd better get back on the other side of my desk." She smiled then pressed her lips together as Steve moved confidently back to the chair.

"I'm sorry."

"Don't be. I'm certainly not." Tori wanted more than anything to feel his arms around her again, to offer the much-needed support and comfort that she felt there. "I wish things could be different, that we could go on with our relationship, but we both need to consider who stands to be hurt. The teachers and students are counting on us."

"If you missed their message in the van yesterday, I think they are unanimously pushing us together."

She felt her cheeks turn pink, just as they had when he'd playfully smacked her with his sloppy kiss.

"I'm not arguing what you're saying, Tori. It kills me to agree with you, but you have to realize that they're going to be cooking up romance, even without encouragement."

"Then maybe it's our job to convince them otherwise."

"How do you plan to do that?"

"Find a date for Homecoming," she said defiantly.

She'd already asked Robert yesterday, and true to form, he accepted. She only hoped she wasn't sorry later.

"I thought you said Mr. Football is just a friend."

"I told you that, but I didn't tell everyone. Let them think what they want." Tori glanced up, the smoldering flame of jealousy in his eyes surprising her. "I earned the nickname honestly, Steve, and I don't plan to let my feelings for you interfere with my job. So no more PDA's, off or on school grounds."

"Let's put this in perspective, Tori. The school board president isn't bothered to know his ex-girlfriend and his cousin care for each other, the teachers seem to think we're perfect together, and you not only want discretion, but you want to pretend it doesn't exist?" The derisive grin told her he wouldn't go along with her plan. "Then why didn't you push me away before that kiss?"

"Because I'm human and I wanted another kiss. Because I do care about you and I did need a moment of comfort. But as the principal, it was wrong. And I'm sorry. I won't compromise what's right, even when I'm the one making the mistake." She stood and looked him in the eye. "I wouldn't even go for the A when it went against what I believed."

His expression was one of pained disbelief. "Did you tell your previous staff about your tainted GPA?"

"Not right away, I didn't. And I didn't date Robert, even though I wasn't his supervisor. Robert's a kind-hearted teddy bear that everyone loves…admires. He's going to be my date at Homecoming Saturday night."

Steve just shook his head. "Didn't take long, did it?"

"I saw the writing on the wall yesterday and asked him. He knows about the incident in the van."

"But not about us?" Steve didn't raise his voice, but he lowered it to an even more alarming tone.

Tori was silenced by the dark, angry expression on Steve's face and she quickly turned away. "We had ten seconds to talk alone, Steve. I couldn't go into it. I'll explain it to him."

Steve walked to the door. "I'm sure anyone named 'Squeaky' is true to her word."

He walked out of her office and closed the door behind him. She had expected his reaction, and understood how he felt, yet it didn't take away the sting.

Tori completed her paperwork on Jane Doe— "counseled on personal issues with pregnancy."

She filed the report and turned her computer on, to add a few ideas—her doctoral thesis notes. While it processed she went to get a glass of tea. When she returned to the computer, the screen saver read, "Hello, this is God. I will be handling all of your problems today. Your help is not needed. Just remember ASAP—Always Send A Prayer. Have a good day." Tori simply stared at the words on her computer screen.

How had that gotten onto her computer, and what was the person trying to tell her? She had control issues? She marched into Steve's administrative office to find it empty.

"He had to take his daughter for her athletic physical, remember?" Carly answered when Tori questioned his absence.

"Oh, yeah."

"Can I help you with something?" Carly looked wide-eyed and innocent. Maybe she had put the message on her computer?

"Was there anyone on my computer yesterday, Miss Westbrook?"

"No one. The glass men were in there, but no one was near your desk. I made sure of it. Is something wrong with it?"

Tori shook her head. "I'm going to sit in on a class. Buzz if you need me."

The afternoon faded away in a blur.

The insurance company agreed to pay to clean her house and make the necessary repairs. She ordered a new laptop to replace her computer, which would make it easy to keep up with her work. It was time she get back to work on her thesis before she forgot the direction she had been going on it.

Tori spent another week at her grandparents', still waiting for her new furniture to be delivered.

She didn't see much of Steve the rest of Homecoming week. He pointedly kept his distance from Tori, staying in his classroom except for lunch duty or when she called him in specifically about school business. He'd even stayed in the background during the Homecoming pep rally Friday after school, looking like a secret-service agent hiding in the shadows.

Robert arrived just in time for the football game

Saturday afternoon. Dressed in baggy jeans and a University of Northern Colorado Football Championship sweatshirt stirred plenty of attention and raised hopes that scouts were here to recruit Tommy Jiminez.

"Show-off," Tori said as he approached.

He looked down at his shirt and patted the football across his chest. "Never hurts to get our alma mater a little free advertising."

"No argument there," she said, noting the attention they were drawing.

"So this is home, huh?"

She nodded. "Some things never change. Segundo is one of them." She hadn't been able to tell Robert about Steve when he'd called the previous night, and now felt an urgency to do so. "I meant to explain why I invited you today."

"Hey, you don't need—"

"I do." She didn't think that after all of these years that Robert would ever think of them as more than friends, but she didn't want any more misunderstandings.

"No, you don't. I saw the look on Mr. Military's face when I saw you Monday. How scared should I be? He's not a SEAL, is he?"

Tori laughed. "No, he's not a SEAL. Army Corps of Engineers. I'm not sure exactly what he did, but he's our upper-level math teacher and quite good at building things."

"And the district has one of those squeaky-clean clauses, huh?"

"Well, yes. But we aren't dating."

"Of course not." Robert stood with his arms crossed over his barrel chest and his eyes glued to the players on the field. "Your quarterback has a powerful arm."

"Tommy's a bright spot in the school. Unfortunately, he has a cousin with a lot of problems. We suspended the cousin last week. I hope he doesn't pick tonight to make his own homecoming."

"Afternoon," Steve said, and they both jumped slightly. He offered his hand to Robert. "I'm Steve Remington. We met on Monday. Nice of you to come today."

"Hi, Tori," Kyle said, tossing his football into the air. "Dad, can I get some licorice?"

"Sure, we'll get you and Matt a treat in a few minutes."

Robert winked at Tori and smiled. "I thought Tori would never come to her senses. I've been asking her out since college. But you know how she's a stickler for rules." He got a goofy look on his face and rolled his eyes.

"Yeah, I've noticed that," Steve said, crossing his arms over his chest, too. "So you've known each other for quite a while, then."

Tori should have been offended that Steve thought she'd lie to him, but she really wanted to laugh instead. Despite temptation Tori kept her eyes glued to the game.

"What's it been, Squeaky, fourteen years? This move may just be an answer to your prayers."

"Really?" Steve said, acutely wary of Robert. There was no denying an affection between Robert and Tori, but Steve wasn't sure if it was more than the "admiration" which Tori claimed.

Tommy threw for a touchdown, and the band started playing, ending their chance for conversation. The fans showed good sportsmanship and the students were well-behaved. Three quarters later, the Coal Valley Mountain Lions charged into the school, victorious.

Steve waited for the field to clear before locking the gates. He ran his kids home, changed clothes then headed back to the school to help serve at the Alumni Dinner. Tori and Robert had arrived just ahead of him, and Carly Westbrook approached him. "I thought Tori wasn't bringing a date."

"When did she say that?"

"A couple of weeks ago." Carly looked to him as if he could do something about it. "Well…"

Steve shrugged. "Well what?" He continued setting the silverware on the disposable plastic tablecloths.

"Do something. You're not going to give up this easily, are you?"

Steve looked across the room and saw Bulging-Muscles-Robert carrying a dishwasher tray full of glasses while Tori set them at the places. He looked at Tori leaning against Robert's sturdy frame and laughing together like best friends. Maybe that truly was the case. Maybe they had been friends so long that, to Tori, dating would be a mistake. "I think you've misunderstood something, Carly."

"I know there's feelings between you two," she whispered as the cafeteria lights went out and replica Victorian lampposts were plugged in. "Don't you try to deny it. We have to think of something to get them apart."

Dinner progressed smoothly with record-setting attendance. It made him feel good to see the support of former graduates after the effort Tori had made to get them here. Maybe Tori could pull off her parent support group, after all. Steve kept water glasses filled, while Tori and her date carried platters of meals to guests, welcoming them with her beautiful smile. When her grandfather strolled in, pushing her grandmother's wheelchair through the door, everyone clapped, and he could see the emotion in Tori's eyes.

As the younger generation moved from the cafeteria into the gym, so did the four vintage lamps. Steve carried the last one down the hall. Tori had donated them, insisting that she'd had them in her garage doing nothing but collecting dust. He could attest to her fabrication of the truth, but he admired her generosity and kept quiet. She had stepped into the planning committee at the final stages and sent out the invitations to alumni without cost to the school budget.

"We need an administrator in the main bathrooms immediately!" Carly's voice boomed over the intercom and Steve couldn't believe she'd really followed through with a plan to separate Tori and Robert. Steve plugged the last lamp in and headed across the gym floor, hearing screams echo through the halls.

Chapter Fifteen

Tori and Steve arrived outside the girls' rest room at the same time to find a handful of hysterical girls surrounded by a crowd of frightened onlookers. Tori had made it to the inner circle of upset students first. "What happened?"

Four girls displayed a vast array of mottled hands and spotted dresses. "Miss Sandoval, there's blood in the water, and it won't wash off." Again the girls shrieked, tears streaming down their faces, trailing mascara with them.

Steve pushed his way to the victims. "What?" He looked at the girls' hands. "Blood wouldn't stain your skin like that. You're okay. Calm down."

One girl went into hysterics, clinging to Steve like a character in a sixties horror movie. "You're fine, Shelley," he said, patting her shoulder.

Tori looked at him; puzzled. "Is it rust?"

He shook his head. "Probably powdered drink mix. Check all of the faucets. See if they've all been rigged."

"Powdered drink mix?" the girls said in unison, smelling their hands.

Tori looked at him like he was crazy. "In the faucets? Who could have…?"

"Check the girls' rest room and I'll check the boys'."

Just as Steve started into the bathroom, two boys rushed out holding up green hands.

"Is this what all the screaming is about?" Corey asked as he exited the rest room with mottled hands, laughing. "It's just a little color. What are they all upset about?"

The other kid pushed Corey. "Moron, nobody wants green hands on Homecoming night. Man, look at this, I look like an alien. If I find out who did this…"

"Alex, in the rest room with me. Corey, don't you move from that spot. I want to talk to you next." Steve followed Alex inside and turned on all of the faucets. They were all filled with color. "Alex, was anyone in here when you came in?"

"Just Corey Moronhead." He shook his head and looked at his hands. "What am I going to tell my date? My hands will probably glow in the dark."

"Was Corey at the sinks when you got here?"

Alex looked at Steve like *he* was the alien. "I don't usually look at anyone in here. I don't know where he was. He was in here. How do I get this off?"

The faucets continued to flow green. "We'll find somewhere for you to wash, but I'm sorry to say it'll probably take a few days to wear off. Be glad it's just your hands. When I was in military school, the guys filled the showerheads. Even our hair was red."

"You did this to someone?"

Steve shook his head. "No, I had nothing to do with the shower prank." He wouldn't admit that he was involved in the retaliation, however mild it seemed compared to walking around with red from head to toe. "Check with the kitchen staff. See if you can use the sink in there."

Steve pulled Corey into the rest room after checking the trash can for evidence. "Corey, let me see those hands again."

"It's no big deal, Mr. Remington."

"To you maybe, but to those girls whose dresses are ruined, and to Alex who feels pretty embarrassed to be seen with green hands, it is." He crossed his arms over his chest. "I'm sure that whoever did this was clever enough to wear gloves so he didn't stain his own hands...." Steve strolled past each sink, turned the water off, removed the spout screen and turned the water on again, allowing the clumps to wash out. He noticed Corey stuff his hands in the pockets of his dark blue slacks. "In any case, I'm sure we'll find the gloves somewhere in the building. I bet that those criminologists from the state could even lift prints from the latex."

"Yeah?"

"Yeah, I saw it on *CSI* a while back. It's pretty tricky, but I bet they could do it." Steve wanted to laugh. "I know an apology for my carelessness in guarding the building today isn't going to help much, but I hope you'll accept it, anyway." He offered a hand to the young man, shocked that he fell for it.

"It's okay, Mr. Remington...."

Steve lifted Corey's hand and turned it palm up, revealing several spots of red on Corey's wrist, right where gloves might end. "It's not okay, Corey. Why are you pulling these pranks? Someone is going to get hurt one of these times."

"What pranks?" He pulled his hand from Steve's grasp. "I didn't do anything else."

Steve watched as the color faded away and the water appeared clear. He motioned for Corey to get to the sinks. "Put the screens back on the faucets, Mr. Claiborne. You'll come in and scrub the sinks clean after school Monday."

"Okay," he said cheerfully.

"Oh, don't think you're getting off that easily," Steve said. "You still have to deal with Miss Sandoval."

Tori assigned Robert to keep everyone out of the bathrooms and asked the teachers to send the kids back to the gymnasium. "Make sure no students leave the building until we have a chance to talk to them. Daria, would you find a bathroom that isn't affected, please?"

When Steve came out of the bathroom with Corey she could see the frustration on Steve's face. He looked at Robert and back to Tori. "We need to talk in your office."

"I'll be right there," she said, lagging behind to apologize to Robert for putting him to work.

"Is this the kid that tore up your house?"

"No, Miguel is probably hiding out in Texas with

his dad. This prankster is the son of a school board member. Fun, isn't it? I'd better call Dad and get him here to have a visit."

Corey again claimed he didn't have anything to do with the sprinklers at the football game or the fire drill.

Gaining little satisfaction from his responses, Tori assigned him three days of in-school suspension and restitution to all of the victims.

"I'm not paying for their stuff."

"Their families worked hard to save money for to-night, Corey," Steve reminded him.

"Just because my dad has money doesn't mean I have to pay for their date."

"If their dresses don't come clean you *will* be paying for them. In any case, you can't get them clean again before the dance, or their pictures, or any of that. You've already ruined their night. Paying may make you think twice before you try anything again."

"My dad will call you!"

"I have already called him and he's on his way now. You'll sit in this chair while we wait." Tori motioned for him to sit in the main office near the window so they could keep an eye on him.

"Aw, come on, it was just a joke."

Tori closed her office door, leaving the main office open to the hallway. Robert met them in the hall, and with a nod from Tori, he stayed to make sure Corey didn't move while Steve and Tori went to remove the spout screens in the girls' rest room.

By the time the night was over, Corey's father was

as upset as his son, but not for the same reason. He fully supported the restitution, the in-school suspension and cleaning up the mess. "I'm not sure that's enough to send a message."

"Dad!"

"We brought Miss Sandoval here to make changes, and this is nothing more than a slap on the hand."

"This is his first referral, and is within the discipline guidelines, Mr. Claiborne," Tori reminded him. She could see he still wasn't happy.

"How about if he earns the money for the restitution by working with the custodians for a month?"

"Aw, come on, Dad. I'll pay for it out of my allowance."

"What allowance?" His dad's message hit Corey between the eyes. "This kind of behavior is going to stop before they take our school away from us. Is my meaning clear, Miss Sandoval, Mr. Remington?"

Tori looked at Steve, not sure what to say. "Mr. Claiborne, may we speak with you before you leave? Corey, have a seat back in the main office, please."

Corey closed the door behind him and sat in the chair. Tori took a deep breath. "Mr. Claiborne, I appreciate your support in this incident, but I don't feel that it would be fair to make an undue example of Corey because he's the son of a school board member."

"I want everyone to know that I'm not expecting favoritism. We don't even know who pulled the fire alarm or what punishment he received. With the break-in at your house, I'd think you'd be a lot tougher on these kids."

Tori laughed. "We don't know for sure who pulled the alarm, and I don't feel a fire alarm is reason to over-react. The suspect who broke into my house has a war-rant for his arrest. And I am trying to discipline your son according to school board policy, Mr. Claiborne. While I understand your desire for a tough-love ap-proach here, this was a prank that did no bodily harm. If you, as a parent, want to remove his allowance and strongly suggest that he get a job, I respect that. But as the principal, I will not assign such discipline for a first-time offense."

Mr. Claiborne stared at Tori for a minute then looked at Steve and nodded. "All right, then. If you're afraid to show a backbone to the students, we'll handle this through the proper channels." He stood up and left.

"ASAP," Steve said.

"Already have," she said with a smile. "So it was you that sent the message."

"Guilty as charged."

Tori sighed, and Robert showed up in her office. "How did that go? Dad didn't look too happy."

"It was the strangest and saddest experience in my career," Tori said. Steve filled Robert in on the discus-sion.

"No one said taking the high road was easier," Steve added.

"What would you have done differently?" Tori said. "Just for the sake of discussion."

"For Corey, set up a behavior modification plan. Of course, I still suspect he had a hand in the other incidents. I think you hit the nail on the head. He wants attention—no matter what he has to do to get it."

"Lets get back to the party and enjoy what we can. We haven't heard the end of this one."

Monday morning Tori called the students in to ask for receipts for damages, sensing the rumbling of contention from the school board. The phones were too quiet following an incident like this. When Brody's call came that afternoon, she wasn't surprised.

"Tori, the board wants to meet with you and Steve to see if we can settle this disagreement with Bob Claiborne."

"What time?" Tori pulled up her calendar on screen. She hoped it was soon, to get it off her mind. The staff had more critical issues to focus on, like educating students.

"No argument?"

"No," Tori said. "There's no avoiding it. I'll say what I need to say in front of the board."

After dinner, she and Steve walked into city hall for the special board meeting while Kyle and Kelsey stayed with Tori's grandparents. Tori repeated what she'd said to Corey's father in her office Homecoming night. "Contrary to rumor, I have no aversion to being known as a tough disciplinarian, but I will not be unjust."

"Steve, could you give us your opinion on this matter?" Brody, though the president of the board, didn't seem to lose sight of the fact that they were all friends and neighbors.

"I'm afraid I'm not impartial on this incident, members of the board. I support Miss Sandoval's disciplinary action as being fair and appropriate for the severity of the incident."

"What do you mean that you're not impartial?" Bob Claiborne asked from the floor, as he had removed himself from his official position for this meeting.

Tori's heart beat faster, hoping Steve wouldn't say anything hinting at their feelings for each other.

Steve looked at Bob, then to his cousin. "There's no easy way to say this, as we have no proof, but I suspect, and have from the beginning, that Corey is responsible for other minor incidents at the school."

"What else?" Bob jumped from his seat. Everyone started talking at once.

Brody fumbled to find the gavel. Failing, he whistled and got everyone's attention. "Bob, sit down. Let Steve finish talking."

"We've had four minor incidents at the school this year. We suspect the sprinklers were intentionally turned on during the football game, the fire alarm was pulled while Corey had no class scheduled, the microphone was disassembled and, now, the colored water. We haven't been able to prove anyone was purposefully involved with the first two and have no idea who could have taken the microphone apart, so we have not disciplined anyone. My suspicions are based fully on observation of recent changes in Corey's atti-

tude and behavior and not on physical evidence. There-
fore, I fully support Miss Sandoval's action. We both
tried talking to Corey and cannot get a confession from
him for the previous issues. It's not fair to give him
harsher punishment than any other student simply to
make an example of him."

Tori could hear the ticking of the clock, the room
was so quiet.

Several minutes later, Brody asked Bob if he wanted
to pursue a change in the discipline policy. He shook
his head. "I don't see a need for change. I would agree
with Mr. Remington's observances of Corey. We don't
seem to be living on the same planet these days. I appreciate your candor, Steve. What else would you suggest to reach Corey?"

Steve looked to Tori and nodded. She explained,
"Mr. Remington has discussed some ideas with me for
a behavior modification plan, Mr. Claiborne. We would
be happy to meet with you, your wife and Corey to set
that up. I don't mind sharing the plan with you, but I
don't feel it's necessary to share your son's specific
needs with the board at this time."

"We could come anytime, Miss Sandoval. Thank
you."

After the meeting closed, Mr. Claiborne set up a
time to meet with Steve and Tori.

Over the next few weeks, Corey's behavior seemed
to improve, and after a formal apology to the girls
whose dresses were ruined, the students quit giving
Corey a bad time about the prank.

* * *

The first day back after Christmas vacation Steve asked Corey to come to his room after school. Steve had spent extra time with Corey, making an effort to help him find productive ways to express himself.

"You like to draw, don't you, Corey?"

"Yeah."

"Do you draw cartoons?"

"Sure."

He motioned for Corey to follow him down the hall. "We have this white dry-erase board that we seldom use. What would you think of drawing a cartoon on the board each week or two. Something having to do with academics or school spirit."

"Really?" Corey's eyebrows arched above his glasses and Steve realized what was different about him. His geeky glasses had been replaced with round wire-rims over the holiday break.

"Did you get new glasses?"

The fifteen-year-old beamed. "Yeah, pretty cool, aren't they?"

"Yeah, maybe I should get some like them. Who's your eye doctor?"

"I dunno. My mom made the appointment, but we got the glasses at that place on the corner of Main Street in Trinidad."

"I'll check them out." Steve hadn't had time to find an eye doctor since he'd left the army. He'd tried to read a novel over the break. After the third headache, he'd given up trying. It was time to give in and get glasses.

"Be sure you use the correct markers, and nothing derogatory to the school or any individuals or the project is history."

"Cool. I'll sketch some ideas tonight and show you tomorrow, okay?"

Steve nodded. "Sounds great. Have a good evening."

He watched Corey dash down the hall, thinking of how Corey had begun to shine lately. He definitely had a different outlook than he'd had at the beginning of the year.

"Well, aren't you clever?" Tori said, the underlying admiration in her words captivating him. "He's really turned around."

Steve tucked his thumbs into his pockets and turned to face her. They hadn't talked about their relationship in nearly two months, and he was weary from the denial. She had turned in an A for his college course, and Steve had hoped to return exclusively to the classroom and pursue their relationship.

The school board, however, had other ideas. Since Jerry wasn't able to return yet, they asked Steve to stay on for the remainder of the year since they had turned down Tory's request for a campus monitor to handle security.

One look at Tori in the pink suit and he wanted to kick himself. *ASAP. Take away the attraction, Lord.*

"He just wanted a little attention, like you said. His parents seem to be making a better effort to encourage his interests rather than their own dreams for him, and according to Bob, he's even talking to them now."

"That's an accomplishment for any teenager," she said with a smile. "God's just full of miracles these days, isn't He?"

Tori's soft voice held a rasp of excitement, and Steve looked at her before he could stop himself. Focus, Steve, focus. He tried to speak, and it sounded like he'd just eaten peanut butter.

Tori touched his shoulder. "Are you okay? Did you catch a cold over Christmas?"

"I'm fine," he croaked again. He walked to the drinking fountain and took his time. "What else has God been doing?"

"The school board approved the new attendance policy. Starting next week we add twenty minutes on to every day, a slight revision from our proposal. But we'll have an extra week off in February. So with the ranchers' help, the kids will all be in school during testing week."

"Great." He hadn't thought he could make it through two weeks without seeing Tori at Christmas, but he had made it, thanks to building the house. He'd considered asking her out to see it, but feared it was too soon. "Did you have a good break?"

"It was quiet, but busy. I finished cleaning and setting up my house. I worked on my thesis. Mom and Dad agreed to move home permanently, so that was an unexpected gift, though I think we've about finished *Abuela*'s therapy. She took about six steps without her walker on New Year's Day."

"That's wonderful, Tori." He looked at her, surprised to see a tearful smile. "Hey, no tears."

"I know, but joyful ones are okay, aren't they?" She stood motionless, and Steve saw the tear trickle down her cheek.

"You look like cotton candy in that suit. One tear could melt you away," he said, his emotions raw. He glanced up and down the hall, making sure they were alone.

"Steve." His name rolled off her pink lips like a whisper in the dark.

"Don't wear that suit when I haven't seen you for sixteen days and expect me to ignore you," he grumbled.

"Good night, Tori," Carly said as she left the office. "Oh, hi, Steve. I didn't know you were still here. See you two tomorrow."

"Have a good evening, Miss Westbrook."

"Night," Steve said, half-thankful for Carly's timely exit. "See you tomorrow, Tori. I should get the kids early this evening, give Bette a break."

"Oh, I thought we could have a pop before we leave, and discuss our schedules for the next couple of weeks."

He glanced at her again, sorry he did. "I think we'd better make it tomorrow—and wear something really ugly, would you? Give me a break." Steve backed away, ready to run down the hall as fast as he could.

"Was that a compliment?" she asked with a smile.

He stepped close and lowered his voice, hoping it didn't give out again. "It's as close to one as I dare get right now."

Chapter Sixteen

Steve hammered the finishing nail into the crown molding, contemplating the fact that Tori was picking her parents up at the airport this morning and he wanted to be there with her. He wanted her here with him even more, and he hadn't even told her about the house yet. Soon it would be time to paint walls and order the flooring, and he wanted more than anything to offer Tori the chance to help make those decisions. But until Jerry Waterman made a decision on whether he'd return or retire, the school board's hands were tied. Officially, Jerry had another month to make his decision.

That meant Steve needed to hold out for a while longer. If Jerry returned, Tori may not want to stay. And if he retired, the district might need to fill two positions, superintendent and principal.

"Brody, I need a hand with the upper cabinets on the other wall," Steve yelled down the stairs. "Are you at a stopping point on the trim?"

"Be right there," his cousin answered.

"Dad." Kelsey ran up the stairs ahead of Brody. "How come you haven't shown Tori the house?"

Brody walked past Steve with an ornery grin. "Yeah, explain that one to a ten-year-old."

"I'm eleven now," Kelsey corrected.

Brody looked at her and hit his head with the palm of his hand. "No way. That wasn't your real birthday, was it? I thought you just wanted to party."

"You're a dork, Brody."

The banter allowed Steve time to come up with an explanation. "If I showed it to her, it wouldn't be a surprise."

"Does Tori like surprises?"

Steve shrugged. "I'm not sure, but I hope so."

"Are you going to ask her to be our mom?"

"Shhh. That's a really big surprise, from everyone. No one but you and me can know that one. Can you keep it a really big secret?"

Kelsey looked over her shoulder, her eyes open wide, as if afraid she'd blown it already. She nodded.

Brody had turned his back on them and started singing, but Steve could see his shoulders moving up and down from laughter.

"Kels, go find Matt and Kyle, would you? I'm going to get lunch on soon."

He heard the front door slam and looked at Brody. "You're not helping matters much."

"Hey, she started asking me questions. I sent her to ask Dad."

"Can't you hurry Jerry up on his decision?"

"He has another month. Besides, the board would like to see how smoothly this experiment with the attendance for CSAPs goes, too, so they're not in a hurry to make an offer. Sorry."

Steve lifted the kitchen cabinet above the space for the stove and Brody helped line it up and hold it steady while Steve nailed it into place. After they had fitted all of the cupboards into position, Steve leveled and secured them.

"This looks really good." Brody stood back and assessed the kitchen area. "Personally, I don't think you should wait."

"You know how she is about that rule in the district policy. Why don't you just get the board moving on changing it? Then I could ask her to marry me."

"And who's going to recommend we look at it? I bring it up and every suspicion about you two is out in the open."

"You bring it up in preparation for Jerry's decision. If you have to hire for either or both positions…"

"What are the chances we hire a super whose spouse could qualify for principal?"

"Pretty good."

Brody looked at him like he'd lost his mind. "I'll think it through. And you think about my advice—ask her to marry you, show her the house and voilà, happily ever after."

"I don't want her to stay here if she doesn't want to."

"Take it from one who knows, Tori Sandoval doesn't stay anywhere she doesn't want to be. You want her, you'd better be making an airtight plan, because you won't find another Tori."

"If you don't get that rule changed, I won't be the only one looking for another Tori." Steve saw no point in arguing with Brody about her. He'd never met Anna, and it was just too hard to explain that the two women Steve had loved could be so much alike. Brody would never believe it, anyway.

Steve had silently observed a change in Tori in the few weeks since her parents' return. He admired the way Tori encouraged and stood by Nicole Tiponi as her pregnancy became evident to the rest of the school. Every week, Nicole sat in church with Tori and her family, which now included Tori's parents, as well.

Valentine's Day came and went before Jerry Waterman announced his retirement as principal and superintendent, sending the school board into a frenzy of special meetings.

"Let's all relax," Tori said at the teacher meeting. "This does not mean trouble as far as the state is concerned. Our job is to continue to teach, maintain a stable atmosphere for the students and keep them in school. We're only two weeks away from testing. Next week they're off. Then we have one week to get their brains back in gear and then it's test time."

Daria looked at Tori "What will your answer be if the board asks you to stay?"

"Let's not put the cart before the horse, Daria. They're waiting for testing to be completed before making any decisions."

She looked at Steve, expecting at least a glance, but he didn't even look her way.

Lately Steve had seemed preoccupied. He came to work on time, did his job, attended the assigned events and said little else not related to business. Tori wondered if she had pushed him away too many times. Had her drive for perfection finally frightened him away? She'd lived through being alone before and she tried to convince herself that she could again, but it hadn't been working.

She reviewed the testing schedule with the teachers and reminded them to invite students to have breakfast at school every morning of testing. "Since juniors and seniors aren't tested, they can meet in the library for study hall during that time, but make sure they understand, they will not be allowed past the main corridor for any reason."

The teachers began complaining.

"We have no choice in the matter. It's state rules."

"Yeah, Squeaky." Daria chuckled. "We'd hate to break a rule."

"Have nontesting students been in the classrooms in previous years?"

After a long hesitation that said everything that needed to be said, Jason Hunt chimed in. "Some. The bus students had nowhere else to be. We were just happy to have them show up for school."

Tori shook her head and rested her head in her hands. "No, no, no. The rules may seem like a pain, but we have no choice but to follow them." No wonder they'd had such low scores. If the state learned there were nontesting students in the classes those scores could have been trashed. "Bus students must either arrange for alternate transportation or plan to stay in study hall. *No* juniors or seniors will be allowed in the classrooms." Tori answered more questions then looked across the table. "Do you have anything else, Steve?"

"Nothing."

"That's it, then." The teachers gathered their schedules and threw away the napkins and paper cups from their refreshments. "How are you feeling, Tracy?"

"Great. Just can't believe how tired I am."

"You look wonderful. I hear Nicole finally came to see you. Thank you for taking time to share your pregnancy experience with her. That's one area I'm little help in—counseling."

"It was a little odd at first, but I'm glad I did. Sounds like she's still struggling with whether to keep it or give it up for adoption."

"I'm sure it's not an easy decision. I'm encouraging her to listen to God's direction." From the corner of her eye she saw Geoff and Steve talking. No one seemed to be in any hurry to leave today.

Tracy finished her water and tossed the cup into the trash. "I'd better get going. Have a good evening, Tori."

"You, too." Tori began cleaning up, catching bits of the ensuing conversations.

Daria discussed basketball with Fred's replacement, Victor Montoya. Larisa stood in the hallway talking to

Corey Claiborne about joining the drama club to help with the artwork for the sets. Why he hadn't joined on his own was a wonder. She guessed he liked the feeling that someone noticed and appreciated his talent.

"We drove past your new house last weekend. Looks like you're almost ready to move in," Geoff said to Steve.

"Not quite," Steve said in a hushed tone.

"That's a nice area. We've been looking around for a piece of land…." Geoff didn't seem to realize that Steve's attention wasn't on their conversation. Finally Steve asked him to stop by next time they were in the area and he'd show him the house. That seemed to satisfy Geoff, and soon the rest of the teachers filed out of the cafeteria. Tori walked down the hall to the office wondering how she had missed the fact that Steve was working on a house.

"Tori." Steve closed the door to the main office and locked it behind him. "We need to talk."

She turned her back to him, trying to hide her tears.

"I wanted to surprise you. I didn't plan on you finding out this way."

"I'm surprised," she said, blinking the moisture away.

He moved closer and Tori held up her hand to stop him. "Why didn't you tell me?"

"I was waiting for the right time."

"Well, this wasn't it." She bit her lip. "Despite the restrictions, I thought we had a relationship building. And you couldn't even tell me you're settling here."

"That's exactly why I didn't tell you. I didn't want you jumping to the wrong conclusions. I started all of this last spring, before we even met. I needed to reinvest the money from the sale of the house in Maryland."

She rocked back gracefully on the heels of her black pumps and sat on the corner of her desk. "All the more reason to have told me up front. I wouldn't have thought anything of it then. But now…" She hugged her arms to her body. "…Now it looks like you're trying to trap me here."

"I wouldn't do that. You've had a lot on your mind. You asked me to keep my distance, and…" He looked at her with a critical squint. "And I didn't want to frighten you away with exactly the impression you have."

The phone rang, and Tori considered letting it go, until she noticed the time. "It's either Bette wondering where you are, or my parents wondering if I'm coming for dinner."

He looked at his watch and then out the window. His was the only vehicle in the parking lot, which meant he must be late getting the kids again. Tori answered the call, turning her back to him. "No, thanks, Mom. I have some leftovers, and I need to proofread my thesis tonight."

She shook her head. "Yes, Steve's still here…." She was quiet. "We had a teacher meeting," she said, slightly irritated. "No, I'm not bringing him over to meet you tonight." She'd come close to losing her temper, but was hanging on by a thread. "Because," she said, closing her eyes. "Because he has to pick up his kids, and I'm sure they already have plans for dinner."

Steve smiled as he considered accepting, just to meet them. She must have read his thoughts, as she shook her head no. "No, Mama, not tonight."

He looked at her with amused wonder. When she finally ended the call, he called Bette, letting her know he would be there in a few minutes. "We're staying at the new house tonight. It's missing all the comforts of home, but I'd like to see what you think of it. Kelsey has been dying to invite you up for supper."

Tori crossed her arms in front of her, that look of defiance in her eyes. "How'd you keep them from telling me?"

"I told them it was a surprise, which it was, in a way. I've been putting off choosing the paint and the flooring." He placed his hands on her waist and pulled her to her feet. "I've been praying about us since the day I met you, Victoria Sandoval. As many times as I've tried to convince myself that the last thing I need in my life is another career-oriented woman, God shows me over and over just how much I need you." He looked at his watch again. "And as much as I need you, I really need to go get the kids. Won't you please come with us?"

"Another night, maybe. There's a lot to think about…."

Steve backed away reluctantly. Much as he hated to, he had to leave her to think all of this through on her own.

After the kids were in bed, Steve looked out the vaulted windows of the living room at the lights in the valley. He thought back to the day he'd met Tori. She'd had her phone clipped to her hip, a chip on her shoulder and a determination to stay in her successful school doing a terrific job and climbing the ladder to the top of a school district somewhere in her dreams.

He had resented those dreams until he'd seen for himself what a difference God's gifts made when used to their fullest. He couldn't believe her strength and composure in the face of adversity. Not once had she turned her back on someone in need, a job to be done or taken the easy way out of any situation. He looked around the spacious home he'd built and realized he, too, had struggled to regain control over the past few years. He came here to spend more time with his kids, and ended up working a full-time job and going back to school. One more test and he'd be done, but he resented the hours earning it had taken away from his kids.

"Daddy, I'm scared," Kyle said as he padded across the unfinished floor in his pyjamas. "Will you come sleep with me?"

"Sure I will," he answered, lifting Kyle into his arms. Suddenly he was very thankful that Tori had turned down his invitation. "That's what a daddy's for."

Chapter Seventeen

Tori wondered if she'd ever stop running from the fear of abandonment. ASAP. I've tried praying for freedom from my idiotic fears before. I don't need to bother God with it again. She reheated her leftovers and turned her computer on, realizing that her parents were just down the street. And this time they weren't leaving. Why had it taken them so long to realize that they were needed right here at home?

How could they have overlooked the fact that there were needy people next door and hungry people down the street? They didn't have to travel thousands of miles to serve others.

The phone rang, and Tori let it ring. She was tired of hang-ups and telemarketers interrupting her evenings. If it was someone who really needed her, they wouldn't hang up. After the fifth ring, Tori decided it wasn't a salesman, and answered.

"Miss Sandoval…" the young voice whispered tightly. "Help."

"Who is this?"

Her breathing was rapid. "Nicole."

"Oh, no." Tori looked for her cell phone. "Tell me what's wrong."

"I c-c-can't."

Was she okay? Had something happened to the baby, or was she simply frightened of something? "Is Miguel there?" Tori picked up her cell phone and entered the sheriff's department phone number.

"Yes," she whispered, and Tori hit the send button. "But he's gone now."

"Are you okay, Nicole?"

"The baby." She started crying again. "I think I lost it."

"I'm calling the sheriff, Nicole, and an ambulance. Hang on, I'll be right there." Thankfully she had been taking Nicole to church each week and dropping her off back at home so she wouldn't need to take time to look up her address.

"Sheriff's Department. How can I help…?"

"This is Tori Sandoval. We need police and an ambulance at the Tiponi home on Elk Drive. I'm leaving soon to—"

"Is there an emergency?"

"Yes, I'm trying to explain. Miguel Jiminez is back in town. He may have beat up his girlfriend, Nicole Tiponi. Would you send an ambulance to her house. He broke into my house in October and there's a warrant for his arrest." She locked the back door and checked all of the windows.

"Her address?"

"I don't know the house number, but it's on Elk Drive, south of the highway."

"Just a moment while I relay your call. We can look up the exact address." Tori heard the dispatcher repeating the information into the radios. She grabbed her keys and coat. "Nicole, I'm on with the sheriff's dispatcher. They're sending help."

Nicole didn't say anything. "Nicole? Are you okay?"

She heard squealing tires outside and rushed to lock the door. Red and blue lights flashed through the drapes. "Nicole, if you can hear me, I'm on my way. I have to hang up now. I'll be right there."

"Tori," a man's voice said as he knocked on the door. "It's Luis Martinez."

She opened the door and hurried outside. "Nicole Tiponi just called. Miguel's back. I don't know if he beat her up, but she thinks she's losing the baby. He left her house. I need to get there."

Luis rushed back to his squad car and motioned for her to join him. "Get in. I was just down the highway when I heard the call. I wanted to make sure Miguel wasn't on his way here to get you personally this time. Buckle up."

As he pulled out, Tori relayed the information Nicole had told her. "I just got home and started heating my dinner when she called." Tori had never driven the curvy two-lane highway so fast, and couldn't believe it when Luis pulled them into the Tiponi driveway a few minutes later.

Marcus stumbled outside into the tiny yard, holding his stomach. "Miz Sandoval, he beat her really bad this time."

She stopped next to Marcus. "Did he hurt you, too?"

He pulled his hands away, revealing a fresh wound. "Said he came to finish what we started in school. He's on his way to your place."

She took him by the shoulders and led him inside to the sofa. "Well, thank God I missed him. Lie down here and wait for the ambulance."

Luis followed them inside carrying a medical bag. "Here. Cover it with this towel for now. Where are your sisters?"

"Nicole's in the bedroom. Mom has the little ones at the store with her. They left right before Miguel got here. He must have been watching."

Tori found Nicole unconscious. *Oh, dear Lord. What has he done to her? Dear God, take care of Nicole and Marcus and help the police find Miguel before he hurts anyone else.* She shook Nicole's arm and placed her face next to Nicole's. "She's still breathing," she told the EMT as he came into the room. Tori backed out of their way. "She's four months pregnant. Before she lost consciousness she said she thought she lost the baby."

"How long has she been unconscious?" he asked.

"I was on with the sheriff's dispatcher. It was almost

seven-thirty." Tori looked at her watch. "Maybe six, seven minutes now."

He looked at his watch and jotted a note on the athletic tape strip on his pant leg. "Thanks. Why don't you go on out to the other room." While the EMTs provided treatment and prepared Nicole and Marcus for the drive to the nearest hospital, Tori called her parents, relieved when her father answered. She told them what had happened, that she was okay and ordered them not to go outside, not to answer the door and to call the sheriff if they heard any noise outside.

"Tori." Luis touched her arm. "Nicole wants you."

"Hold on, Daddy. She's awake." She moved to Nicole's side and took her hand as the medics loaded her into the ambulance. "Nicole, I'll be at the hospital praying for you."

"Careful, Miz Sandoval."

"We need to get her to Trinidad." Together the EMTs lifted Nicole inside and closed the door.

Tori watched the ambulance drive away with lights and sirens. "Daddy, Miguel is very dangerous. He knows which house is mine, but I wouldn't be surprised if he knows where *Abuela* and *Abuelo*'s house is, too."

"We'll be on the lookout, honey. You take care of yourself."

"I love you, Daddy."

"We love you, Victoria. His guardian angels will be watching over all of us. By the way, Steve called looking for you."

"Thanks. I'll call him."

She hoped he hadn't heard of the trouble already.

"Tori," Luis told her, "I need to wait for Marcus and Nicole's mother to get here. Trinidad sent a couple of officers to stake out your house. Do you have a key hidden that they could use to get inside?"

"At my grandparents' house. I just told them to be wary of any noise outside. If the officers are there now, I can let them know it's okay. It would be nice if they could look around outside their house, too, as long as they're there. Make sure Miguel isn't hiding in the piñon trees."

He relayed the information to the officers over the radio and asked for their location. They hadn't made it past the coal ovens at Cokeville yet. "Call me when you get to their house. I don't want any more innocent victims tonight." He turned to Tori. "Wish I'd have thought to ask where the kids' mother was going shopping. I could have called and had the manager detain her."

Tori called Steve, hoping Miguel hadn't decided to go after Steve, too. It took forever for him to answer, and her imagination went wild.

"Steve…" She forced her emotions aside, just long enough to tell him had happened, though she longed for him to be there to hold her and tell her everything would be okay. "I'm fine. I'm waiting for Mrs. Tiponi to get back from shopping so we can tell her about Marcus and Nicole. Then I'm going to the hospital."

"Would you like me to go with you?"

"Thanks, but you have the kids to take care of. Be careful, Steve. We don't know Miguel isn't mad at you, too."

"Very few people know I'm up here, so I'm not too concerned. But I have a lot to be careful for. I love you, Tori."

"Yeah, me, too."

He laughed. "You're not alone?"

"No, I'm with Luis. I'm fine."

"Does that mean you feel the same about me? A simple yes or no will do."

Tori could almost imagine Steve's protective embrace around her. "Yes." She closed her eyes and waited for his reaction.

"Yes!" the warmth of his smile echoed in his voice. "Call me later, and if you need a safe place, I'm here."

Twenty minutes later the officers called back. "Sorry for the delay. We found Miguel. Someone called in a crash at the school. This kid had to have been high on something. He wrapped himself around a tree next to the school. He's not going to hurt anyone else."

"Guess God made sure justice was taken care of," Luis said as he took pictures of the scene at the Tiponi home.

Tori nodded. "And sad as it is, He took care of Nicole at the same time." She didn't know how else to live with herself for convincing the teen to keep the baby, than to accept that God would also heal Nicole and Marcus's pain. Would Miguel have beaten Nicole if she'd had the abortion? Did he even figure it out himself, or had Nicole defended her decision to him? Tori sat at the kitchen table with her head in her hands. *Father, again You remind me that You will take care of our problems if we bring them to you. Give these children another chance to experience Your mercy, Lord. Be with Marcus and Nicole tonight and always.*

It was an hour before Nicole's mother arrived, and Tori was frantic to know what was going on at the hospital. She had called back her parents and Steve to tell them that Miguel was dead and they could rest easier.

Tori spent most of the night at the hospital with Mrs. Tiponi and the younger children. Marcus's cut required minor surgery and Nicole lost the baby. Both would be in the hospital for several days to recover.

"Miss Sandoval, I can't thank you enough for staying with me tonight. And for coming to this job. We drifted away from the church when my husband left and I took my other job. I'm so grateful to you for showing Nicole God's love. We really didn't know what to do about the baby, and by the grace of God, we know it's in His loving hands now. I'm selfishly praising the Lord that Miguel can't hurt anyone else."

"You're not the only one feeling selfish right now, but I don't think God wants us to feel anything but joy that Nicole's and Marcus's injuries looked much worse than they were."

School was a somber place for the rest of the week. Tori spent most evenings either at the hospital or watching the younger Tiponi children while their mother spent some of her free time with Marcus and Nicole. Mrs. Tiponi's words stuck with Tori through each minute of the day. Over the years she had sat with several families through students' tragic illnesses, accidents and deaths, and not a one had thanked her.

Miguel's funeral wasn't well attended, but Steve and Tori went to offer support to his cousin, Tommy, who was traumatized more by Miguel's violent actions than his death. "How am I supposed to face everyone at school?" he asked after the burial.

Steve wrapped an arm around his shoulder. "With your head high. They've known Miguel as long as you have. The other kids know you didn't approve of what he was doing, and they know you're not like him. When you come back after spring break next week, they'll be over the shock, too."

"Do you think we could have that cop come in and talk to the school again about the dangers of drugs?"

Tori looked to Steve. "It might be a little soon now, but maybe toward the end of the school year. We'll see."

Tori spent the weekend revising her doctoral thesis. Her experience at Coal Valley Secondary School had shaken both her educational and religious beliefs. "My statistics reveal frightening commonalities between both affluent and low-income latchkey children," she wrote. "The commitment of parents to become involved and active in their child's education is paramount to the success of a teacher's ability to educate that child."

As she sat in on Steve's trigonometry class for his final evaluation Tori couldn't help but wonder who had inspired Steve to become an educator. He had a natural connection to the students. Most higher-level math classes were sparse, but Steve had kids suffering through college-prep math courses just to make it into his entertaining classroom. The school would lose a valuable asset when he became a principal. And if there was one thing he was even better at than teaching, it was leadership.

After his class ended they discussed the evaluation. Later in the day she gave him a copy of the written version for his signature. "That is the last evaluation I'm ever going to do on your teaching skills."

His laugh rumbled. "Professionally, maybe."

Tori returned his smile. "I meant that you're going to be an administrator next year, so I won't have to do your evaluations."

"Does that mean you'll consider doing personal evaluations?"

"Talk about an overachiever. I'm not even going to address that comment."

"Fine. It can wait for later. Speaking of achievements, did you finish rewriting your thesis?"

"I did. I defend it next week."

"And then I'll have to call you Dr. Sandoval."

She looked at him oddly. "Sounds funny, doesn't it?"

"I don't know. What do you think?" He smiled, mockingly coy, then ran his finger along her jaw.

"Maybe you'd rather be called Dr. Sandoval-Remington."

"You're forgetting one little rule."

"One of these days, I'm going to burn that rule book."

Silently, Tori realized God had healed the emotional scars of her childhood and shown her the rewards of her hometown. She'd learned to forgive herself, and her parents, for the differences that had kept them apart.

Steve couldn't help but notice the change in Tori's attitude. Still, he wasn't so confident about their future. She'd been through so much here, he wondered if it was fair to ask her to stay. It had been another challenging week. Though the teachers weren't pleased with the nitpicky rules of the CSAP tests, thanks to Tori's heavy hand, they had one-hundred-percent attendance on all three test dates. Such an accomplishment was unheard of.

Though she'd joked around about taking his last name, Steve had learned never to take anything for granted when it came to Victoria Sandoval. She was used to victory, had been since birth, he suspected. It went with the name. He only hoped that soon, they could share a victory, in His name.

Chapter Eighteen

Brody called Steve at the new house Monday afternoon of spring break. "I've been trying to reach you all day. I think you may want to be at the school board meeting tonight."

Steve had just finished plastering the final wall in the basement and wanted to get the painting done over spring break. He hadn't counted on doing any schoolwork this week. "What's up?"

"Just be there." Brody hung up.

What could be wrong? Tori's evaluation had gone well. He had taken a larger role in discipline and budget issues recently. Maybe they had questions about those that they wanted clarified. "Kids, I have to go to the board meeting tonight. Pick up your toys so we can grab a bite at the café before I go. He cleaned up and called Bette to see if she could watch the kids for a few hours rather than having to take them back to the ranch.

When he walked into city hall that night, Brody

asked for approval of the agenda. Bob Claiborne made the motion, but asked to add an item prior to the discussion of replacing the superintendent and the principal.

Steve closed the door quietly and sat in the back row, then looked to Brody, who gave a quick nod and stifled a smile.

Further down in the minutes Jerry Waterman's retirement was discussed, with the recommendation that the board try to fill the two positions. If they were unable to for some reason, Jerry was willing to remain in the superintendent position part-time.

Tori had worn her cotton-candy-pink suit tonight and left her hair loose, something she rarely did at work. She looked all of twenty-five, and Steve marveled at her accomplishments. She had to be one of the youngest principals in the state. She sat in the second row with the principal from the primary school and several of the staff from CVSS, and again he wondered what was on tonight's docket that he needed to be prepared for.

The treasurer reviewed the budget, noting that the allotment for salaries had dropped considerably due to Fred Esquival's retirement, and would again drop with Jerry's vacated positions.

Bob read his full proposal to rescind forbidding personal relationships among staff, confirming Steve's hopes. Another board member moved to take an immediate vote to avoid any delays in the hiring process. The vote passed unanimously. Steve wished he knew who to thank for speeding the process.

He and Tori had a lot of time to make up for, and his patience was long gone. He started planning a dinner out with Tori right then.

The next item on the agenda was Tori's update on the new attendance policy and a summary of CSAP testing. The board and staff congratulated her on a successful plan.

Bob Claiborne raised his hand when Brody asked for new business. "I'd like to make a recommendation to fill our vacant positions." He started to explain his reasons, and Brody stopped him.

"Discussion comes after the second, Bob."

"Second," Mrs. Primrose said.

Brody opened the issue for discussion, and Bob started in again. "Last year the state board of education wanted us to take a hard look at our student retention, which was then in a bad way. We haven't had one transfer out this year, and have almost a dozen students wanting to transfer into CVSS next year. They wanted us to consider changes in staff, and by necessity, we made changes. We've had a lot of upheaval this year with those changes, and so far the kids have made the adjustment to Miss Sandoval's and Mr. Remington's leadership. I feel we should ask both of them to return, in whatever capacity necessary to keep them both. If Miss Sandoval will qualify for superintendent and Mr. Remington the principal's position, we'd have it made."

Though many families weren't present because of calving season, the majority of the staff and a few of the more involved parents nearly filled the room. Brody didn't look too surprised by the motion, and after the applause stopped, he read from his pad of paper. "We would need to move to fill the positions temporarily, pending the completion of their respective licensures. Do we have a second?"

Mrs. Primrose again seconded the motion.

"All in favor of offering the position of secondary principal to Steven Remington, raise their hand." Every board member voted yes. "Note that it was a unanimous vote, please."

"And now for the position of superintendent to be offered to Victoria Sandoval. All in favor raise their right hand." Every hand raised.

"I will meet with Tori and Steve to discuss the particulars."

After the business had concluded Brody asked for any additional comments.

"We would be fools to let these two get away!" Mrs. Primrose said. Steve could see Tori's blush when she turned her head.

"Steve," Brody called. "You have anything to say?"

"Well, since I haven't even sent out an application for the job yet, I'm honored to be asked to take the position. I will need to get back with the board after my licensure test scores come back, of course, and there is one more factor I need to consider before accepting." He walked to the front of the room and paused next to the row Tori was seated in. "I've had the privilege of working with Victoria Sandoval this year as an administrative intern. Professionally, I couldn't have had a better mentor. Personally, I'm very thankful to the board for removing the restrictions of falling in love with the principal." Everyone laughed. Everyone except Tori.

It appeared he'd finally shaken her. "Tori, I need one answer before either of us dare accept the job offer."

Her cheeks turned pink, and Steve wondered if he'd made another mistake following his impulse to get their relationship out in the open.

"I don't recall any question," she said.

He rolled the ring around in his pocket. He decided a board meeting probably wasn't the best place to propose, and backed off from his initial plan, though he had been carrying an engagement ring with him for days, hoping the right time would present itself. "I was wondering if you'd like to go steady."

"Steady?" The blush on her face deepened, as if she was now embarrassed that he'd not proposed, after all.

"Yeah, steady, as in to every Homecoming and prom for the rest of our lives."

She smiled. "That could be a while you know."

"I'm counting on it." He held his breath, wondering what to do next. He'd never proposed marriage in front of an audience before.

She transformed into teenager mode when she got up from her chair, placing her hand sassily on her hip. She gave him her "don't mess with me" stare. "You ask a girl to go steady, you have to have a ring, Rem...

come on, follow the rules." She smiled and stepped past the primary school principal.

"So if I have this," he said, holding up the diamond ring, "we could officially date?"

Her eyes opened wide. "Oh, Steve, I wasn't serious," she said breathlessly. "What are you doing carrying something like this around for?"

"Just waiting for you to realize you've found your way home."

"I have." She nodded and took a step closer. "I should have known better than to argue with God. If you're serious, I have a week open in July."

Steve paused only a moment before taking her into his arms and making up for lost time. He wasn't surprised when the kiss ended and their audience cheered on.

The meeting ended with congratulations from each board member, and a slap on the back from Brody. "You two are going to have a very busy few months. I take it you're both considering the offer, then?"

Tori smiled. "Just so long as you have a better maternity plan than the school I just turned down. It just so happens we have family close by who would like to watch a baby for us." Tori kissed Steve again.

"Give her a ring, and she's already rewriting the rules," Brody teased.

Steve smiled. "Marriage is full of compromises, but the one subject we've already agreed upon is that kids come first…. Um, right after the wedding, that is."

* * * * *

Dear Reader,

This generation is supposed to learn more at a younger age, and with that comes the expectation that teachers and educators wear more hats than ever before. They're often expected to fill the shoes of social worker, friend, advocate, mediator, parent liaison, police, counselor, coach and last, but most importantly, teacher. And when administrators move from the classroom into leadership, the expectations double.

Twenty-six years ago I married into a family of educators. I first met my future father-in-law as a student anxiously sitting in the junior high principal's office. Throughout the years he grew to appreciate the many expectations of his job. Whether it was to discipline an ornery student, intervene with disagreements between student and teacher, or rush to the school in the middle of the night because fire alarms had gone off, the job never ends.

Now my husband is a principal, and the inspiration for *Finding Her Home.* I'm continually reminded God is present in all schools, with administrators, teachers, staff or students, giving His children courage and patience to face what each day brings. And with quiet faith can come countless opportunities to make an impact on those in need.

Please pray for all of our schools and our educators, that all will be willing to speak up when God commands.

I love to hear from my readers. Please feel free to contact me at P.O. Box 200269, Evans, CO 80620 or at csteward37@comcast.net. Don't forget to visit my Web site at www.carolsteward.com.

Carol Steward

Love Inspired®

TO HEAL A HEART

BY

ARLENE JAMES

Finding a handwritten letter at the airport offering
forgiveness to an unknown recipient put widowed
lawyer Mitch Sayer on a quest to uncover its
addressee...until he sat down next to Piper Wynne.
His lovely seatmate made him temporarily forget his
mission. After the flight, he kept running into Piper,
whose eyes hid painful secrets...including the fact
that the letter was written to her!

Don't miss

TO HEAL A HEART
On sale January 2005

Available at your favorite retail outlet.

A MOTHER FOR CINDY

BY

MARGARET DALEY

Widow Jesse Bradshaw had her hands full with her young son, her doll-making business and a gaggle of pets. She couldn't imagine adding anything more to her already crowded life—until jaded Nick Blackburn and his daughter moved in next door. Jesse was all set to use her matchmaking skills to find a mate for the workaholic widower, but what would she do when she realized that she wanted to be little Cindy's mom?

THE LADIES OF SWEETWATER LAKE:
Like a wedding ring, this circle of friends is never ending.

Don't miss

A MOTHER FOR CINDY
On sale January 2005

Available at your favorite retail outlet.

Take 2 inspirational love stories FREE!

PLUS get a FREE surprise gift!

Mail to Steeple Hill Reader Service™

In U.S.	In Canada
3010 Walden Ave.	P.O. Box 609
P.O. Box 1867	Fort Erie, Ontario
Buffalo, NY 14240-1867	L2A 5X3

YES! Please send me 2 free Love Inspired® novels and my free surprise gift. After receiving them, if I don't wish to receive anymore, I can return the shipping statement marked cancel. If I don't cancel, I will receive 4 brand-new novels every month, before they're available in stores! Bill me at the low price of $4.24 each in the U.S. and $4.74 each in Canada, plus 25¢ shipping and handling and applicable sales tax, if any*. That's the complete price and a savings of over 10% off the cover prices—quite a bargain! I understand that accepting the books and gift places me under no obligation ever to buy any books. I can always return a shipment and cancel at any time. Even if I never buy another book from Steeple Hill, the 2 free books and the surprise gift are mine to keep forever.

113 IDN DZ9M
313 IDN DZ9N

Name	(PLEASE PRINT)	
Address	Apt. No.	
City	State/Prov.	Zip/Postal Code

Not valid to current Love Inspired® subscribers.

Want to try two free books from another series?
Call 1-800-873-8635 or visit www.morefreebooks.com.

* Terms and prices are subject to change without notice. Sales tax applicable in New York. Canadian residents will be charged applicable provincial taxes and GST. All orders subject to approval. Offer limited to one per household.

® are registered trademarks owned and used by the trademark owner and or its licensee.

INTLI04R   ©2004 Steeple Hill

Love Inspired®

UNDERCOVER BLESSINGS

BY

DEB KASTNER

Returning to her childhood home was the only way
Lily Montague could keep her injured child safe—little
Abigail had witnessed a friend's kidnapping and was in
danger. Kevin MacCormack, called "guardian angel" by
the girl, was helping her daughter learn to walk again.
But Lily didn't know the strong but gentle man was
an undercover FBI agent, there to protect them both.
When his secret was revealed, would it destroy the
fragile bond that had formed between them?

Don't miss

UNDERCOVER BLESSINGS
On sale January 2005

Available at your favorite retail outlet.

www.SteepleHill.com

LIUBDK